Sniper
the ear

MW00772641

Before Bolan could put out a distress call, a faint popping sounded from atop the peak behind him, followed by an ominous *whoosh* and the harsh glare of two igniting flares. The clouds turned a bright shade of ochre that illuminated the ridgeline, exposing Bolan and O'Brien.

"Go!" O'Brien feebly reached for the compress and pushed Bolan away. "Now!"

The flares touched down, landing close enough that their sparks made the Americans an even clearer target. Two more rounds rained down on Bolan and O'Brien. One glanced off the Executioner's M-16 mere inches from his trigger finger. The other tore through O'Brien's neck, just above his flak jacket. The recon officer went limp, blood spurting from a severed artery.

Given the trajectory, Bolan knew the shots were coming from the distant peak behind him, well beyond the range of his assault rifle. It also seemed a safe bet that there were at least two snipers.

Bolan had to make a quick decision. Staying at O'Brien's side meant certain death, but venturing any farther along the ridgeline would only court the chance he'd trip another land mine. That left one option.

The Executioner took it.

MACK BOLAN ®
The Executioner

The Executioner
Don Pendleton's ®
KILLING GROUND

A GOLD EAGLE BOOK FROM
W⦿RLDWIDE®

TORONTO • NEW YORK • LONDON
AMSTERDAM • PARIS • SYDNEY • HAMBURG
STOCKHOLM • ATHENS • TOKYO • MILAN
MADRID • WARSAW • BUDAPEST • AUCKLAND

Recycling programs
for this product may
not exist in your area.

First edition August 2010

ISBN-13: 978-0-373-64381-3

Special thanks and acknowledgment to
Ron Renauld for his contribution to this work.

KILLING GROUND

Copyright © 2010 by Worldwide Library.

Printed in U.S.A.

They are dead; but they live in each Patriot's breast,
And their names are engraven on honor's bright crest.
                                    —Henry Wadsworth Longfellow
                                              1807–1882

Every soldier who fights for freedom and justice
deserves honor and peace in death. Anyone who
threatens this right will have to answer to me.
                                              —Mack Bolan

THE
MACK BOLAN

LEGEND

Nothing less than a war could have fashioned the destiny of the man called Mack Bolan. Bolan earned the Executioner title in the jungle hell of Vietnam.

But this soldier also wore another name—Sergeant Mercy. He was so tagged because of the compassion he showed to wounded comrades-in-arms and Vietnamese civilians.

Mack Bolan's second tour of duty ended prematurely when he was given emergency leave to return home and bury his family, victims of the Mob. Then he declared a one-man war against the Mafia.

He confronted the Families head-on from coast to coast, and soon a hope of victory began to appear. But Bolan had broken society's every rule. That same society started gunning for this elusive warrior—to no avail.

So Bolan was offered amnesty to work within the system against terrorism. This time, as an employee of Uncle Sam, Bolan became Colonel John Phoenix. With a command center at Stony Man Farm in Virginia, he and his new allies—Able Team and Phoenix Force—waged relentless war on a new adversary: the KGB.

But when his one true love, April Rose, died at the hands of the Soviet terror machine, Bolan severed all ties with Establishment authority.

Now, after a lengthy lone-wolf struggle and much soul-searching, the Executioner has agreed to enter an "arm's-length" alliance with his government once more, reserving the right to pursue personal missions in his Everlasting War.

Safed Koh Range, Afghanistan-Pakistan Border

Fifty miles southeast of the Afghanistan capital of Kabul, Mack Bolan steeled himself against the harsh, cold wind that swept up through the moonlit mountains, stirring a clot of low-hanging clouds that partially obscured the steep, jagged slopes stretching before him. He was nearly ten thousand feet above sea level, positioned along a battle-scarred ridgeline just below the highest peak in this stretch of the Hindu Kush, lying prone on a bed of pine needles. Under better conditions, he would have had a clear view of the trails below, along which, according to all available intel, Taliban forces would most likely attempt to slip into the country from covert bases in the tribal lands of neighboring Pakistan.

The intermittent cloud cover made this an ideal night for the terrorists to make their move. To tempt them farther into the open, an attractive bait had been set two miles to the north, atop a plateau several thousand feet below where Bolan held his vigil. There, U.S. and NATO forces had begun to erect a new base for their joint military operations. It was a familiar *modus operandi* for the Taliban to take advantage of such situations, staging predawn raids in hopes of capitalizing on uncompleted fortifications manned by security personnel not yet acclimated to their new surroundings.

In this case, however, the half-built site was merely a red herring. Once the Taliban crossed the border and closed in on its target, their advance would bring them into the crosshairs of a half-dozen Special Ops teams lying in wait at key points along every known access route. Bolan was one of those who would likely sound the first alarm. If he had his way, by the time the ambush was underway, he would have already made his way downhill to lend a hand in helping crush those from whose ranks America had been subjected to the moment of infamy now known, with grim simplicity, as 9/11. Granted, it would take more than one such victory to eradicate the black-turbanned sect once and for all, but after weeks of making little headway against the terrorists, both U.S. and NATO forces were anxious to boost their morale and at least match the recent success of their host confederates, the Afghan National Army.

The Executioner had come to Afghanistan intent on a solo mission against the Taliban, but once apprised of plans for the ambush—which Pentagon spin doctors had optimistically christened Operation Rat Trap—Bolan had quickly realized that prowling alone through the mountains would more likely draw friendly fire from the commando squads than bring him face-to-face with the enemy. He'd grudgingly allowed himself to be thrown into the established mix, and when he'd set out for his lofty surveillance post, it had been in the company of a recon specialist from the Army's 25th Infantry Division deployed at Bagram Air Base.

The man at his side, as the stakeout dragged into its third hour, was Captain Howard "Howitzer" O'Brien, a beefy, gray-haired veteran halfway through his third tour of duty in Afghanistan. Prior to that, the Cleveland native had served in the Gulf War, and his cumulative experience had brought with it a hardened cynicism surpassed only by the officer's apparently incessant need to vent his notions as to how the U.S. military brain trust had mismanaged both conflicts.

"Y'know, if we'd done things right from the get-go, we wouldn't be stuck here doing this kinda shit," O'Brien murmured as he, like Bolan, peered downhill through night-vision goggles that, for the moment, did little more than deflect grains of sand periodically whipped up by the late-October winds.

"Back in '91 we had Hussein and his fucking Imperial Army dead to rights," he went on. "All we had to do was march into Baghdad and finish the job. But what do we do instead? We call it quits and head home so those scumbags can regroup and pick up where they left off. Real smart, huh?"

It was an old argument, one Bolan had tired of the first few dozen times he'd heard it. When he didn't respond, however, O'Brien took it as a cue to forge on.

"Then, *boom,* ten years later we blow in here to Binladenstan looking to kick some Taliban ass for 9/11. We rout 'em out of Kabul and have 'em right where we want 'em—running scared up here into the mountains. But do we finish the job? Hell no. Instead we get ourselves sidetracked going back after Hussein. By the time we yank him out of his hidey-hole and see that he gets a necktie party, *these* dipshits have retrenched themselves so we gotta come back and start from square one again. You see a pattern here?"

Bolan wasn't about to let himself be dragged into the officer's diatribe. He kept his eyes trained on the mountains below, looking for signs of movement through the shifting clouds. The only visible stirring was a gentle rippling on the surface of a small glimmering mountain lake situated at the base of a steep slope extending downward from his position. There'd been a time when the entire length of the slope had been a sheer, vertical wall of solid rock, but years of bombing, first by the Soviets and then the U.S., had pulverized sections of the precipice, turning them into collapsed mounds of loose rock and gravel. The ripples were caused by the occasional plop of small stones pulled down into the lake by gravity.

"What, you think I'm exaggerating?" O'Brien taunted. "Or maybe you think Washington knows what they're doing and aren't just dicking around for votes and kickbacks from whoever's making the money off this fiasco. Is that it?"

Bolan remained silent. Much as O'Brien's diatribe rankled him, it also took him back to a time when he'd taken issue with his government to the point where he'd gone rogue. It had been a dark period in his life, and though the wounds had healed, the scars remained.

O'Brien broke the silence.

"You know I'm right," he said.

Bolan felt his patience wearing thin. He also sensed that O'Brien wasn't about to let up until he got some kind of response out of the man he knew only as Special Agent Cooper—one of several code names the Executioner used to safeguard his identity as well as that of the covert agency he worked for.

Finally Bolan turned to the captain and raised his goggles long enough to level the officer with a cold look.

"I like politicians about as much as I do hindsight," he replied tersely.

O'Brien stared back into his cohort's withering blue eyes and chortled, then flashed a begrudging smirk.

"Touché," he said. "Okay, okay, memo received. I'll shut up."

Given that the officer had been ranting almost nonstop since they'd set out from the makeshift base camp shortly after nightfall, Bolan doubted O'Brien would keep quiet. On the bright side, after glancing along the ridgeline that tapered away to their right, the recon officer finally told Bolan something he didn't mind hearing.

"I'm gonna contact the other teams to see if they've spotted anything," the captain said, rising to a crouch. He reached to his thigh and pulled a checkbook-size Jorson 278 microcomputer from his cargo pocket. "I'll duck in the bushes to shield the LCD."

"Good idea."

O'Brien snickered again, gathering up his M-16. "Just don't rat me out as a hothead when you report back to CIA or whoever the hell it is you're working for," he said. "I've got a pension waiting for me at the end of this, and I don't want it mucked up."

"Deal," Bolan promised as he lowered his goggles.

O'Brien hunched low and headed off toward a cluster of overgrown hawthorn shrubs farther down the ridgeline, his thick-soled boots crunching on loose gravel. Clouds spilled up over the crest and within a matter of seconds the officer had vanished into their ethereal mist. Grateful for a moment's silence, Bolan turned from O'Brien's location and peered through high-powered binoculars at a patch of mountainside near the lake that had been laid clear by the moving clouds. He was focusing on a narrow ribbon of switchbacks when the night air resounded with a sudden blast, followed quickly by a curdling howl.

O'Brien.

Bolan was quick to his feet, forsaking the binoculars in favor of his Army-issued carbine. He raced down the ridgeline, careful to follow the same route O'Brien had taken. He had a hunch as to what had just happened, and when he came upon the writhing officer, his suspicions were borne out. O'Brien's right leg had been severed just below the knee and blood spurted from the mangled stump into a fresh, shallow crater gouged out of the soil.

"Land mine," the officer moaned weakly.

Bolan shed his goggles and reached for the obliterated mess that had once been O'Brien's right calf. He tugged free the largest available scrap of torn pant leg and pressed it against the officer's wound, hoping to staunch the blood flow.

"Try to stay put," Bolan advised. Blood seeped through the compress, warming his fingers.

"Looks like I get that pension sooner than I thought," O'Brien whispered hoarsely. His ruddy complexion had turned ashen, and he began to shiver. Bolan knew the man was going into shock. He shifted his grip and cupped the severed stump with one hand, freeing the other to reach for the microcomputer O'Brien had dropped. The device had a built-in walkie-talkie, and Bolan knew the captain's only chance would be a medevac airlift back to the base.

Before Bolan could put out a distress call, a faint popping sounded from atop the peak behind him, followed by an ominous *whooosh* and the harsh glare of two igniting flares. The clouds turned a bright shade of ochre that illuminated the ridgeline, exposing Bolan and O'Brien. A second later, sniper fire began to chew at the earth around them.

"Go!" O'Brien feebly reached for the compress and pushed Bolan away. "Now!"

The flares touched down, landing close enough that their sparks made the Americans an even clearer target. Two more rounds rained down on Bolan and O'Brien. One glanced off the Executioner's M-16 mere inches from his trigger finger. The other tore through O'Brien's neck, just above his flak jacket. The recon officer went limp, blood spurting from a severed artery.

Given the trajectory, Bolan knew the shots were coming from the distant peak behind him, well beyond range of his assault rifle. It also seemed a safe bet that there were at least two snipers.

Bolan had to make a quick decision. Staying at O'Brien's side meant certain death, but venturing any farther along the ridgeline would only court the chance he'd trip another land mine. That left one option.

Bolan took it.

2

Casting aside the microcomputer, Bolan dived sharply to his left, then rolled on his side until he reached the point where the ridgeline gave way to the steep-pitched incline. He'd abandoned his carbine, as well, leaving both hands free as he went over the side. The dying flares cast light on a few likely footholds and Bolan put them to quick use, lowering himself enough that the next sniper rounds skimmed off the crest and caromed far above his head. O'Brien remained an open target, and as shots continued to rain down, Bolan suspected the assailants were ensuring that the recon officer had joined the ever-growing list of U.S. fatalities in the prolonged Afghan conflict.

Bolan considered his next move. Off to his right, just beyond reach, a young, hearty spruce jutted through a seam in the precipice. The Executioner looked for a way to inch within reach, but there was nothing between him and the tree but a bald expanse of sheer granite. For that matter, all around him there was little more in the way of footholds, and directly below it was a forty-foot drop to a boulder-strewn stretch of land separating the cliff from the small lake. Bolan realized he'd reached a dead end.

Eventually the flares were spent and darkness once again settled over the mountains. The sniper fire trailed off as the clouds fell back on themselves and wisped past Bolan, increasing his cover. He stayed put but shifted his weight until he felt secure enough to free his right hand. Unsnapping the clasp on his web holster, the Executioner unsheathed a 9 mm Beretta.

Much as he loathed fighting battles on the defensive, there was little for him to do now but wait for the enemy to come to him. He stayed put, forcing himself to remain patient.

Bolan's eyes had readjusted to the darkness when a gust of wind swept across the ridgeline, stirring up loose dirt and showering it down on him. Forced to avert his gaze, the Executioner turned his head and glanced downward. Doing so, he caught a fortuitous glimpse of activity thirty yards past the rubble heap trailing down into the lake. Three men armed with assault rifles were stealing their way up the winding trail by which O'Brien and the Executioner had reached the ridgeline. Their backs were to Bolan, but he knew they had to be Taliban.

The Executioner slowly torqued his body to give him more range with the Beretta. When one of the footholds gave way under his shifting weight, Bolan scrambled to keep his balance. Dislodged bits of rock clattered down the facing and thunked ominously off the larger rocks below.

The gunmen down on the trail were about to make their way around a bend that would have carried them out of view when the last man in the column stopped and glanced over his shoulder, raised his AK-47 and shouted to the men in front of him. Bolan didn't need a translator to realize he'd been spotted.

The Executioner had secured himself enough that he was able to unleash a 3-round burst before the other man could fire. The shots were hurried, but one of them struck home and his would-be assailant crumpled to his knees, carbine slipping from his lifeless fingers. When the next closest Taliban dropped to a crouch and drew a bead on Bolan, the Executioner fired again. There were no kill shots this time, but he drew blood and the other man wailed as he staggered backward. The third gunman reached out and quickly pulled his colleague to cover behind an escarpment buttressing the bend in the trail.

Overhead, far up near the top of the peak from which the original shots had been fired, Bolan heard more muffled shouts, followed by the rattle of falling stones he'd been listening for earlier. At least one of the snipers was coming down after him. When the clamor grew louder and small rocks began to tumble over the edge of the ridgeline, Bolan figured the attacker had bypassed trails and was sliding down the loose bed of choss. If that was the case, he'd reach the ridgeline in a matter of seconds.

The Executioner hadn't emptied his Beretta, but he quickly swapped out the semiautomatic's half-spent magazine for a fresh one, certain he'd need all the firepower he could muster should he find himself locked in a cross fire. If it came to that, he knew his chances were slim. The clouds had moved on, leaving him splayed against the rock, every bit as vulnerable a target as O'Brien had been after the land mine had taken him down.

There was no further activity on the trail below him, but overhead Bolan soon heard the tramp of footsteps. One of the snipers had already reached the ridge and was closing in on him.

Bolan was weighing his next move when, about a mile to the north, staccato bursts from several AK-47s suddenly drowned out the sniper's footsteps, followed by return fire from M-16s. The Executioner craned his neck and scanned the terrain where the shots were coming from. Through the drifting clouds, he saw blips of light punctuate the exchange of gunfire close to where one of the Special Ops forces had taken up position. There was only one likely explanation. More of the Taliban had somehow managed to slip past recon and turn the tables on their would-be ambushers.

There was no time to mull over the turn of events. Bolan knew he had to act. It seemed likely that the distant firefight had distracted the enemy closing in on him, and he went with the odds. Holstering his Beretta, he coiled himself against the rock, then pushed off to his right, extending his arms toward

the lone tree growing out from the cliff facing. As his fingers curled around the gnarly trunk, Bolan grabbed tight and
swung forward, building momentum so that when he let go,
he was able to clear the gap leading to the stretch where, as
with the similar slope above, bombing had created a natural
slide made up of pulverized gneiss and granite.

Bolan landed hard on his back amid the loose stone, knocking the wind from his lungs. He struggled to remain conscious
as he felt himself sliding feetfirst down the incline, dislodging
enough rocks and other debris to create a full-scale avalanche.
There was no way to tell if the enemy was firing at him. All
he heard was the thunder of falling rock and the equally loud
reverberation of blood pulsing through his head.

Moments later, Bolan splashed into the lake. The icy water
revived him instantly and as soon as his boots touched the
shallow lake bottom, he bent at the knees and lunged forward,
swimming clear of the larger boulders that had been brought
crashing down behind him. Several rocks glanced off his legs
and right thigh but their force was blunted by the water, and
Bolan was able to stroke his way farther out into the lake.

He remained submerged as long as he could, then, lungs
burning, he angled his way upward and broke the surface.
There he trod water as he gasped for air. He was halfway out
into the lake. A ragged peninsula comprised of fallen trees
and snagged debris stretched toward him from the far shore.
Bolan swam quietly toward it, relying on leg kicks to keep
his splashing to a minimum. Once he reached the trees and
wriggled beneath a moss-covered branch, the Executioner
stopped long enough to catch his breath.

He could still hear gunfire to the north, but there were
shots in the air around him, as well. Bolan wasn't the target,
however, and the most persistent firing came from almost
directly overhead. Bolan peered up and saw a small AH-6J
"Little Bird" combat chopper hovering in place just past the
lake, directing blasts from a side-mounted .50-caliber machine
gun at the Taliban gunmen on the path leading up to the

ridgeline. Bolan couldn't see the trail, but the ridgeline and distant peak were both within view, and there was no sign of fire being returned by the snipers.

There was little Bolan could do to assist those in the chopper, which he recognized as part of the U.S. aerial force based out of Bagram. At the risk of being spotted and mistaken for the enemy, he pushed away from the half-submerged tree and circled around the peninsula, then slowly swam toward the far shore of the small lake. By the time he reached it, the Little Bird had let up on its offensive. The chopper was about to drift toward the precipice when it suddenly shifted course. Its halogen searchlight swept across the lake, falling on Bolan as he pulled himself from the water. The Executioner straggled ashore, half-numbed by the cold water but still able to feel countless bruises he'd sustained since first going over the side of the ridgeline.

The chopper dropped to within a few yards of the embankment. The copilot reached out and helped Bolan up onto the skid.

"Don't think we can squeeze you in here," the copilot shouted over the blare of the rotors.

"I'm fine here," Bolan replied, taking hold of the open door frame as the copter pulled away from the lake, listing at a slight angle to compensate for his added weight.

"There were a couple snipers above the ridgeline," he told the copilot, a Native American in his late twenties.

"Didn't see 'em," the other man told him, "but they'll have to wait. We've got an SOS from Team Five. Taliban popped up out of nowhere and have 'em pinned."

Bolan changed the subject. "You got a dry weapon in there?"

"Sure thing." The copilot reached behind his seat and handed Bolan a foot-long Heckler & Koch MP-5 K submachine gun. The H&K was larger than his Beretta but still fit snugly in his right palm. It packed a greater wallop, too.

Bolan knew that if he kept the weapon close-bolted, he'd be able to fire from the skid with minimal kickback, ensuring better accuracy.

"Where's O'Brien?" the copilot asked.

"Caught a land mine up on the ridge," Bolan told him. "Snipers started in on us before I could call for help. He's gone."

The copilot spit and readied one hand on the trigger operating the Little Bird's outer machine gun. "Bastards!"

The men fell silent as the AH-6J banked into the clouds, using them for cover en route to the distant skirmish. Peering down through the mist, Bolan spotted another of the U.S. commando squads spread out in a column, threading their way along one of the mountain trails. They still had a few switchbacks to negotiate, however, and the Executioner doubted they'd reach the battle in time to be a factor.

Once they emerged from the cloud cover, Bolan saw a CH-47 Chinook hovering in place a quarter mile ahead over terrain that looked much the same as the area he'd just left—half-barren mountains ribboned with narrow trails and pocked by bombs and mortar fire. The Chinook's tail gunner dispensed fire into the brush along a footpath high up near the top of a steep gorge. As they drew closer, Bolan saw a shadowed figure take a hit and plummet into the crevasse. Close by, a second Taliban crouched behind a large boulder, unseen by the tail gunner, drawing a bead on the Chinook with a shoulder-mounted rocket launcher. The Executioner whipped his H&K into firing position and steadied himself on the Little Bird's skid. He cut loose with a single round, striking the boulder. When the Taliban turned toward him, Bolan was ready with a follow-up shot. This time he didn't miss.

"Beat me to him," the copilot shouted to Bolan. "Nice shot."

Bolan pointed to the trail leading away from where he'd dropped the insurgent. "That looks like their way out," he yelled. "Get me as close as you can!"

Bolan's command was relayed to the pilot. The AH-6J promptly swerved right, then dipped toward the trail. Bolan crouched on the skid and waited until the chopper drew closer, then, clutching the MP-5, he pushed clear and dropped to the ground. He landed hard and felt a sharp pain in his right ankle as he lurched away from where the trailed dropped off into the abyss. He struck the rock facing just off the trail and winced as jagged gneiss bit through his shirt, drawing blood. Bolan ignored the wound and braced himself, ready to face the enemy.

3

Aden Saleh cursed as he watched one of his fellow warriors keel into the ravine, the victim of rounds fired from the large American warbird thundering out in the misty night air before him. The hope had been that dust storms forecast for the evening would have reached far enough into the mountains to thwart visibility and keep gunships from responding to the Taliban assault. Such had not been the case, now Saleh's men were paying the price. Yes, they'd managed to take the enemy by surprise and decimate those who would have done the same to them, but the arrival of the helicopters threatened their chances of making a safe retreat to the tunnels through which they'd been able to reach the attack site undetected.

Saleh, a lean, grim-faced man who'd spent nearly half his thirty years rising up through the Taliban ranks, directed his wrath at the hovering Chinook, emptying the last rounds from his Kalashnikov, to little effect. His ammunition spent, he cast the assault rifle aside and yanked a 9 mm Ruger from his waistband. Fifty yards to his left, a smaller chopper had just deposited a soldier on the same footpath where he now stood. The entrance to the tunnel lay between them, but Saleh was closer to it and had no intention of letting the other man prevent him from making his getaway. He whirled and fired, forcing the enemy to cover, then charged forward, mere steps ahead of a strafing round fired his way from the Chinook.

Halfway to the bend where he'd last seen the American, Saleh threw himself to the ground and crawled off the path. He squeezed past a mound of holly just off the trail, then bellied his way beneath a rock formation protruding from the canyon wall. There, in the cold darkness, a manhole-size opening yawned its welcome. Saleh burrowed through the gap and wriggled past a loose boulder, following a narrow shaft to the point where it widened enough for him to rise to his knees. He had no interest in backtracking to reset the boulder that had earlier helped conceal the opening. If anything, at this point he hoped his pursuer would find the entrance and come after him.

Saleh crawled a few more yards, then squirmed clear of the shaft, entering a larger tunnel tall enough to stand in. He quickly brushed himself off, then made his way to the first turn. There he stopped and shoved the Ruger back in his waistband, and pulled from beneath the folds of his shirt a Soviet-made F-1 fragmentation grenade. He thumbed loose the cotter ring, then, pressing the safety lever, he drew in a breath, hoping to soothe the loud clamor of his racing heart. He needed to be able to hear the infidel's approach, so that he would know when to let fly with the *limonka* and turn the entrance shaft into a death trap.

BOLAN STAYED PUT once the insurgent's 9 mm serenade drove him to cover. There was no way for him to round the bend without placing himself back in the line of fire. By the same token, he figured the enemy would be unable to flee any farther without coming his way. Judging from the hail of gunfire spewing from the two choppers, the Executioner also thought there was a good chance any of the retreating Taliban would be dispensed with before they reached him.

As he awaited his next move, Bolan felt the warm trickle of blood running down his shoulder. He shrugged it off and tested his arm, then tried putting his full weight on his right foot. The ankle felt sprained, but not severely enough to hinder him, and he was certain that, at worse, he'd only need a couple stitches in his shoulder. He'd fought on countless times in the past with far worse injuries.

The firefight went on without him, but not for long. Soon the only shots were being fired from the helicopters, and then their guns fell silent, as well. As the Chinook lumbered away, the Little Bird pulled back from its firing position and briefly shone its light on the trail leading to the attack site, then slowly drifted Bolan's way. Once the chopper was within shouting range, the copilot called out to Bolan.

"I think we got 'em all except the one just down the trail from you." The man pointed to Bolan's right. "Fucker dropped to his belly and went Houdini on us."

"He couldn't have just disappeared," Bolan shouted back.

The copilot shrugged. "If you want to check it out, we'll light the way."

Bolan nodded, readying his MP-5. Once the searchlight illuminated the path before him, he ventured around the bend and cautiously made his way forward, slightly favoring his bad ankle. The dirt was etched with bootprints, all of them leading toward the staging site where the Special Ops force had been attacked. It was another twenty yards before he came upon more tracks. The imprints were different from the others, made by boots other than those worn by U.S. troops. All but one set of the tracks led to the ambush site; the other, headed the opposite way, had been made by the man whose retreat Bolan had hoped to prevent. There was a spot where the latter tracks stopped and had been smudged away, along with the other prints. Bolan surmised the reason and glanced to his right, where a small thicket of holly just off the trail had been partially flattened.

The Executioner pointed his gun into the brush while signaling for the Little Bird to shift position. Once the searchlight had been redirected, Bolan saw there was clearance beneath a protuberance in the rock wall that flanked the trail. Cautiously he dropped to a crouch for a better look. Just enough light made its way into the clearance for him to spot the tunnel opening.

Bolan signaled for the chopper to hold steady, then leaned inward. He was about to enter the cavity when he checked himself and stopped, heeding an instinct honed by years on the battlefield.

"I don't think so," he murmured to himself.

Bolan retreated long enough to track down a handful of stones lying along the side of the trail. Clustering them in his fist, he ventured back to the opening, took aim and flung them into the darkness.

Just as the Executioner took a step back there was an explosion. The ground beneath him shook, and he bent at the knees to steady himself as loose debris and frag shards flew out from the opening, laying waste to the holly. Bolan was spared the worst of it, except for a few bits of shrapnel that glanced off his shins.

The blast was short-lived, and in its wake a foul tendril of smoke curled its way through the collapsed remnants of what had once been the tunnel. Bolan could no longer see the opening, but he suspected it would no longer be large enough for anyone to squeeze through.

He was still staring at the damage when the chopper pulled closer.

"Tunnel?" the copilot shouted out to him.

"Not anymore," Bolan called back.

IT TOOK ANOTHER ten minutes for two of the other Special Ops squads to reach the ambush site. With the fighting over, there was nothing left for them to do but help Bolan and the Chinook crew load casualties into the bulky gunship, which had touched down on a plateau eighty yards to the north. It was a sobering task. Of the twelve commandos who'd been attacked, eleven had been slain, their bodies riddled with far more kill shots than had been necessary to take them out. The twelfth commando was also near death and had passed out after confirming that the unit had been attacked by enemy forces who'd clearly used the hidden tunnel to slip undetected within striking distance.

As for the Taliban, six men had been cut down just off the trail near the rocks and dwarf spruce that they'd taken position behind once the first shots had been fired. At least two more were reported to have gone over the side during the ensuing firefight. There was no way of knowing, at this point, how many men had managed to retreat back into the tunnel before Bolan's arrival. The Executioner had inspected the blasted opening shortly after the explosion and confirmed that it was too collapsed and choked with debris to be of use. The AH-6J Little Bird had set out to comb the surrounding mountains in hopes of spotting anyone using another way out of the tunnel. Bolan doubted that anything would come of the search. One of the arriving squad leaders was of a similar sentiment.

"Fuckers are like cockroaches," Captain Rob Kitt said. Kitt was a pallid, broad-shouldered man in his late thirties. He wore a headset-equipped helmet bearing the same camo pattern as his fatigues. "If you can't stomp 'em before they slip through the cracks, forget about it."

"You got that right," another of the commandos said. "Hell, we could punch these mountains with bunker busters from now till doomsday, and there'd still be tunnels left for them to scurry through."

While the last of the U.S. casualties were being carted off, Bolan and Kitt, each clutching a high-powered flashlight, took a closer look at the slain Taliban fighters and their weapons. In addition to AK-47s and the ASG-17 grenade launcher Bolan had prevented from being used on the Chinook, the terrorists had carried out their attack with knockoff G-3s as well as at least two well-worn M-16s that looked as if they dated back more than twenty years to America's campaign to support mujahideen forces opposed to the Soviet occupation.

"Ain't that a bitch," Kitt murmured as he inspected one of the M-16s. "Killed with our own goddamn weapons."

"The Kalashnikovs are just as old," Bolan said.

"Probably scavenged off dead Russkies," Kitt theorized. "We'll haul 'em back to Bagram along with the bodies. Maybe AI can find something that'll clue us in on where they set out from."

When the captain's headset squawked, Kitt excused himself and wandered off, leaving Bolan to muse over the fallen enemy. All but one of them looked to be in their early twenties, wearing black turbans and dark, loose clothing, much of it bloodstained with gunshot wounds. The oldest victim, and by far the most heavily bearded, had a scar along his right cheek and was missing two fingers on his left hand. When Bolan's flashlight caught a gleam of metal beneath the folds of the man's shirt, he leaned over and found an automatic pistol tucked inside his waistband. Like the C3s, it was hand-made, a crude approximation of a U.S. Government Model 1911. Bolan had seen footage of Taliban camps where children worked by candlelight manufacturing such guns as a means of supplementing the insurgents' arsenal. The weapons were notorious for jamming or even exploding when triggered, and Bolan wondered if that had been the cause for the man's missing fingers.

Bolan had begun to search the man more thoroughly when Kitt returned.

"That was Little Bird," he reported. "No luck tracking down any stragglers."

"What about O'Brien?" Bolan asked. "Did they get to him?"

"We've got a problem there," Kitt replied. "They went to ridgeline and can see where he tripped the mine, but there's no sign of him."

Bolan's expression darkened. "He was shot through the neck. There's no way he could have pulled through."

"I'm sure you're right," Kitt said. "My guess is the snipers took the body as some sort of consolation prize."

Bolan's stomach knotted with rage. If he'd had it all to do over, he'd have reacted the same way once the ambush had broken out, but that did little to ease his mind over the notion that Howitzer O'Brien had been left behind to fall into the hands of the enemy.

4

Remnants of a late-season hurricane had wandered far enough inland to lash Virginia's Blue Ridge Mountains with a torrential downpour that left Stony Man Farm, like many other estates scattered throughout the Shenandoah Valley, drenched and wind-battered. Barbara Price, mission controller for the Farm's Sensitive Operations Group, was out helping the blacksuit security force tend to the damage. Sloshing through rain puddles, bundled up warmly against the late-autumn chill, the blond-haired woman gathered up snapped twigs and broken tree limbs that lay strewed in the orchards and added them to a growing heap in the truck bed of one of the Farm's Ford F-150 pickups.

"Could have been worse," one of the blacksuits told her as he stomped on the debris, compressing it to make room for more. Like the others, he had a web-holstered 9 mm pistol concealed beneath his down-lined ski vest and gave no appearance of being anything other than a hired farmhand. "A little colder and the trees would've iced over. If you think this is a mess…"

"We're not out of it yet," Price said, casting an eye on the dark, leaden clouds still massed over the valley. There was more rain in the forecast, and she could only hope the temperature wouldn't dip low enough to threaten the trees further.

As Price gathered up the last of the fallen branches, a rumbling sounded overhead. It wasn't thunder, but rather the familiar, mechanical drone of an approaching helicopter.

Moments later, a small Bell 47 two-seater dropped below the cloud line and approached the camouflaged runway that lay between the orchards and the dormant planting fields.

"I'll let you guys finish up," Price said. She took a large thermos from the front seat of the truck and made her way to the runway. By the time a bulky, middle-aged man wearing a rumpled trench coat had disembarked from the helicopter, she'd filled the thermos cap with coffee.

"Not exactly fresh from the pot," Price said, holding out the coffee. "It's still hot, though, and way too strong."

"Just the way I like it." Hal Brognola, SOG's director, mustered a wan, close-lipped smile. "Thanks."

By the time he'd taken his first sip, Brognola's smile had faded. Price knew it had nothing to do with the coffee. She'd been there to greet Brognola enough times after his return from Washington briefings to know from his expression that the President had just confided in him about some active global threat that would require placing the Farm's elite covert operatives directly in harm's way.

"Afghanistan?" she guessed as they strode from the runway. When Brognola eyed her, she went on, "I spoke with Striker earlier. He filled me in on the ambush."

"The ambush is just part of it," Brognola replied. "And so is the whole matter of this missing soldier."

"Okay, you've got my attention," Price said. "Let's have it."

"It has to do with the Afghan National Army and this whole call for pulling out Western troops." When they reached the main house, Brognola led the way up the front porch, nodding to the blacksuit stationed near the front door. The security agent stepped aside, holding the door open. As they proceeded inside, the SOG director told Price, "At the same time we took this hit at Safed Koh, the ANA was routing a Taliban squad up to the north near Jalalabad."

"They've been on a roll lately, haven't they," Price said. It was more of a statement than a question.

"That's just it," Brognola said. "Up until a few months ago, the pattern was always reversed, with us making headway and having to lend ANA a hand. Then there was all this clamor about pullouts and the Afghans decided they wanted to run their own operations without our input."

"'Meddling' is how I think they put it."

Brognola nodded. At the end of the main hall was a staircase. As they took the steps down, he said, "In any event, since this shift they've been catching all the breaks while we keep running into setbacks. It plays in nicely with their calls for autonomy, but the President and Joint Chiefs think it's all a little too convenient. I'm inclined to agree."

"Same here," Price said.

Once they reached the basement, it was a short walk down to the mouth of a large underground passageway. There was a small electric rail car parked just inside the opening. Brognola took the wheel. Price rode shotgun.

"So I'm guessing it's up to us to see if there's something hinky going on," she said as the car started down the tunnel.

"Correct. The bottom line is this," Brognola said. "If the ANA is legitimately trouncing the Taliban, we want to know how they're doing it. Just as important, we want to make sure they're doing it on their own."

"You think maybe they've cut a deal elsewhere?"

"That's what we need to find out," Brognola said. "I've thought through a game plan, but I'd like your input before we run it past the cybercrew."

"No problem," Price responded, "That's what a mission controller's for."

ONCE ALL THE FALLEN BRANCHES were loaded into the pickup, one of the blacksuits drove from the orchards to the Annex, a large outbuilding located on the far east perimeter of the estate next to a stand of young poplars that had been equally pummeled by the storm. Inside the building, limbs and twigs from the latter trees were being fed into the growling maw of an industrial wood chipper and turned into mulch, one of the by-products that was presented to the outside world as proof of Stony Man Farm's agricultural reason for being. The various enterprises did, in fact, cover a portion of the Farm's sizable overhead, but the site had a more far-reaching agenda. There in the Annex, one floor beneath the thick concrete slab upon which the wood chipper carried out its noisy duties, Price and Brognola had just emerged from the underground tunnel and were making their way to the Computer Room, nerve center for America's best-kept secret in the covert war against those intent, one way or another, on bringing the country to its knees.

"That sounds like the way to go," Price said, once Brognola had laid out his strategy for dealing with the situation in Afghanistan. "We're going to have our hands full, though."

"Fortunately, that's something we're used to," Brognola replied as he opened the door for his colleague.

"I'll apprise Striker while you brief the others."

"Sounds like a plan."

The Computer Room was a vast brightly lit chamber with workstations positioned here and there, a far wall lined with large flat-screen monitors that flashed an ever-changing patch-work of display maps, news feeds and images from aerial sat cams. Three-quarters of the Stony Man cybernetic crew— Aaron "the Bear" Kurtzman, Huntington Wethers and Carmen Delahunt—were on duty, laboring intently at their consoles to provide needed INTEL and logistical backup for SOG commando teams on assignment both at home and abroad. One by one, however, they took note of Price and Brognola's arrival and quickly shifted their attention.

Price exchanged a brief greeting with the others, then excused herself and moved to a corner alcove, where she dialed out on a secured phone line routed through enough code scramblers to sidestep any possible attempt to intercept the call. Brognola, meanwhile, unbuttoned his trench coat and raided the liner pocket for a twenty-dollar Padron, one of two dozen such hand-rolled cigars presented to him by Phoenix Force leader David McCarter upon that unit's successful return from a mission three weeks ago in Nicaragua. There had been a time, years ago, when Brognola would have lit up and shrugged off the gibes of those who took exception to the pungent smoke, but times had changed and the big Fed now contented himself with rolling the cigar between his fingers as he spoke or chewing on it.

"Where's Akira?" he queried, glancing at a vacant station normally commandeered by the cybercrew's youngest member, Akira Tokaido.

"Catnap in the lounge," answered Delahunt, a fiery redhead in her late forties who'd come to Stony Man by way of the FBI. "We started a union while you were out and decided we deserve a little shut-eye when the brain cells overheat."

Brognola rolled with the wisecrack. "Fine by me," he said. "As long as you do it in shifts. Just don't start asking for maid service and mints on your pillows."

"Fair enough."

Wethers, a one-time Berkeley cybernetics professor with neither the knack nor patience for small talk, cleared his throat, eager to steer focus back to more pressing concerns.

"Something came up at the briefing, I take it," he said to Brognola. "Does it have to do with Striker and the Taliban?"

Brognola nodded, shedding his trench coat and draping it over the back of Tokaido's chair.

SOG's two commando units, Able Team and Phoenix Force, invariably handled missions as a group, but Bolan's preference, as it had been when he first set out for Afghanistan, was to work alone, knowing the crew back in Virginia would cover his back. Brognola intended to do all he could to see that the Farm held up its end of the bargain. He quickly passed along news of the Safed Koh ambush, concluding with the update Price had received earlier from Bolan.

"We've had no luck rounding up anyone who left the attack site," he said. "The feeling is they've managed to slip back into Pakistan, most likely with O'Brien's body."

"By Pakistan I take it you mean the tribal region," Delahunt said.

"That's always been our premise, and there's nothing here to suggest otherwise," Brognola said. "The ambushers we were able to recover are with Army Intelligence at Bagram. They're going through personal effects while the bodies are autopsied to see if there's some dietary tip-off as to where they might have been holed up."

"Dietary tip-off?" Kurtzman asked. "That's a new one on me."

"Different tribes, different crops," Brognola said. "If any of them have undigested food in their system, it could be as good as finding fingerprints in a homicide case."

"'Alimentary, my dear Watson,'" Delahunt said, invoking a Sherlock Holmesian British accent. When Wethers shot her a stern glance, she told him, "C'mon, Hunt, a little levity won't grind things to a halt, okay?"

"Does that make it another one of our 'union perks'?"

Delahunt laughed. "Hey, what do you know, Hunt made a funny."

"Okay, people," Brognola interceded. "Can we get back to the task at hand? Following up on this ambush is just our first step. There's a wider picture we need to be looking at, as well."

Brognola paced before his colleagues as he quickly reiterated what he'd told Price earlier regarding concerns about the ease with which the Afghan National Army had been striking lopsided blows against the Taliban while the joint U.S.-NATO effort was being stymied at every turn. When he stressed how the ANA's solo triumphs coincided with growing calls for Western pullouts, all three members of the cyberteam agreed on the need to look for another explanation besides a run of good luck on the part of the home team.

Kurtzman, the crew's wheelchair-bound leader, was the first to respond after Brognola had completed the briefing. "I'll start culling sat-cam databases for signs of Taliban movement along the border," he said.

"Good," Brognola said. "Also see what you can do about getting one of the orbitals to make a few extra passes over that whole stretch of mountains. BASIC would probably be your best bet, but use my name and pull in markers with the National Reconnaissance Office or some of the private firms if you have to."

"Will do."

"You didn't bring it up," Wethers said, "but shouldn't we also be looking into how the Taliban knew where our ops teams were positioned? From the sounds of it, they were right on target when they came out of that tunnel."

"Not to mention they were breathing down Striker's neck from the get-go up on that ridgeline," Delahunt added. "I'm smelling a tip-off."

Price had just wrapped up her call with Bolan and rejoined the group in time to overhear the last exchange.

"Striker's thinking the same thing," she told Wethers. "AI assured him they're looking into it."

"All the same, let's do our own checking," Brognola said. "Did he have anything new to report?"

"A possible break, actually," Price said. "A recon chopper came across someone lying wounded in the mountains near Jalalabad a couple hours ago. He was unconscious with multiple bullet wounds, but he was too far from where the ops team was attacked so they're thinking maybe he's part of that Taliban crew the ANA took out around the same time."

"It'd be nice if that was the case," Brognola said. "Especially if we can get him to talk."

"It sounded to Striker like it's pretty touch-and-go as to whether this guy will even pull through," Price said. "They flew him to Bagram and he's still in surgery. Apparently he's got internal injuries and nearly bled out."

"Let's hope for the best," Brognola said. "We could use a break."

"One other thing," Price added. "Striker wants carte blanche in terms of his next move. He wants to go with the first strong lead on where they took O'Brien's body."

"Not a problem," the big Fed said. "I'm sure that whole situation is weighing on him."

"'No man left behind'? Yeah, I think it's a concern for him," Price said. "Can't say as I blame him."

"Me, either," Kurtzman interjected, "but he was following that same code when he went to help the guys being ambushed. It's not like he was retreating."

"I'm sure he realizes that, but still…"

"C'mon folks," Brognola said, stuffing the cigar in his shirt pocket so that he could have both hands free to roll up his sleeves. "We've got a big haystack to comb through, so let's get cracking."

"Will do," Delahunt said. "I'm wondering, though… Given the situation over there, is the President still looking to make that photo op in Kabul next week?"

Brognola shook his head. "He'll still be going to Istanbul for the NATO conference, but he's scratched the side trip."

"Smart move," Delahunt said. "Last thing we need is the Taliban feathering their turbans with an assassination."

5

Spin Range, Nangarhar Province, Afghanistan

As Brognola was rallying his cybercrew in the Stony Man Computer Room, halfway around the world, high in the arid mountains just north of Safed Koh Range, the enemy the SOG was trying to place in its sights was huddled in an inauspicious farm hut, with dirt floors and windows draped loosely with flaps of leopard skin to fend off the cold winter air. In the center of the room three men sat close together on mats set around a low, candlelit table, warming themselves with hot tea and steamed rice sprinkled with shaved bits of roast lamb. They spoke quietly, barely above a whisper, but their words carried both passion and urgency as they addressed events of the past twelve hours.

General Zahir Rashid of the Afghan National Army, at sixty-three by far the oldest of the three, was out of uniform, dressed like the others in plain shepherd's clothing. There were streaks of gray in his neatly trimmed beard and a glimmer of intensity in his dark brown eyes. A veteran of Afghanistan's United Front, Rashid had come into his own once that group's militia had morphed into the ANA. He was also widely credited as the mastermind behind the string of recent victories Afghan troops had racked up against the Taliban. The previous night, in fact, he'd taken to the field and led the successful defeat of an insurgent squad in the mountains near Jalalabad. However, that one-sided skirmish would never have been possible without the input of the man seated directly across from him.

It was Aden Saleh, a high-ranking member of the Taliban and the warrior who'd eluded Bolan in the aftermath of the Safed Koh conflagration. He'd not only apprised Rashid of the Taliban's movements in the Spin Range, but had also seen to it that the insurgent group stalked its way blindly into an ambush that had resulted in the deaths of all but one of its men. The ploy had been easy enough to carry out, because for the past six months Saleh had been in charge of orchestrating each and every incursion into Afghanistan made by the black-turbanned renegades. Saleh's reasons for betraying his own men were simple. As with any organization, there were schisms within the Taliban. The majority of those who'd fallen in the Jalalabad battle, like most of the others slain by ANA forces over the past few weeks, were part of a dissenting minority opposed to a strategy to regain control of Afghanistan, not by acting alone, but by entering into a covert alliance with Rashid and other rogue ANA generals. This alliance also had outside force whose support, Saleh and his superiors felt, would be essential to ensuring that any coup would not be quickly undone by the U.S.-NATO coalition.

Spearheading efforts on behalf of that outside force was the third man seated at the table.

Eshaq Faryad, a native of neighboring Uzbekistan, had been among the first soldiers to set foot in Afghanistan during the 1979 Soviet invasion, and for ten years he'd remained in the country, doing all he could to help fend off counterattacks by the mujahideen. Years after the Soviet occupation had been squashed, thereby forcing him to flee back across the border, Faryad was back, this time in collusion with some of the same Afghan leaders he'd earlier fought against. As before, his primary objective was to place the country under Russia's yoke. And while Uzbekistan had been awarded its sovereignty following the breakup of the Soviet Union, Faryad's allegiance remained with Moscow, and all these years the bald, clean-shaved man had continued to receive orders—as well as a steady, sizeable income—from the Russian capital's *intelligentsia apparatchik*. In recent years that organization's official title may have changed countless times, but in his heart Faryad still considered himself KGB—SVR to the rest of the world.

The three men had come together to discuss a number of issues, but two in particular weighed most heavily on them in terms of immediacy.

First was the matter of the U.S. soldier whose body had been hauled away from the ridgeline in Safed Koh by the sniper who'd killed him after he'd triggered a Taliban-set land mine. Captain Howard O'Brien's corpse lay just outside the hut, stripped and covered beneath a layer of snow brought down from the higher elevations. His weapons, along with a microcomputer, had been confiscated and what was left of the recon officer's uniform was being washed and mended in hopes some use could be made of it. Meanwhile, the men squabbled over what to do with the body.

Saleh wanted to use the slain officer as barter in hopes of negotiating the release of Azzizhudin Karimi, the low-level Taliban fighter who'd survived the ambush by Rashid's ANA troops the night before in the hills outside Jalalabad. But Faryad and Rashid opposed the idea, taking the sniper's word that the other U.S. soldier who'd been on the ridgeline had to know O'Brien was already dead. They knew there was no way the U.S. would exchange a live prisoner for a dead one. For that matter, Rashid was equally skeptical that they would even be able to use O'Brien to secure the return of the bodies of the men who'd fought alongside Saleh when they'd ambushed the Special Ops team in the mountains of Safed Koh. The Afghan general had already learned from his informants at Bagram Air Base that those victims were in the process of being autopsied at the request of U.S. Army Intelligence.

Saleh had been enraged by the news of such desecration, but he realized it was pointless to argue any further for trying to leverage O'Brien's body as a bargaining chip. This was, he decided, one of those situations when it was best to back off from his position for the sake of maintaining the alliance with those seated across from him. Besides, acquiescence now would likely serve him down the line should a time come when he would need one of them, in turn, to side with him as swing vote on some other matter.

"Very well," the Taliban leader finally relented. "We'll make use of his weapons and uniform and just dispose of the body."

"Preferably in a way that it's never found," Rashid added. "If the Americans are kept wondering about his fate, it will be something of a victory."

"Agreed," Faryad said.

"I'll see to it personally," Saleh said.

"It's settled then," Rashid replied. "Let's move on."

"Before we do, what about the computer?" Faryad asked.

"What about it?" Rashid said. "We don't have the access code. Without that, it's of no use to us."

"We should try to crack the code," the SVR agent suggested. "If we can get into the system, it could prove invaluable."

"If you know anything about hacking, you're welcome to try," Rashid countered.

"I know someone," Faryad said. "I'll look into it."

"As you wish," Rashid said, eager to change the subject. "Now, we need to discuss how to deal with Karimi."

Saleh's simmering resentment got the better of him. Before he could check himself, he found himself blurting, "If you'd finished him off when you had the chance, there would be nothing to deal with."

A sudden tension filled the room. Rashid's face reddened as he stroked his beard and then busied himself with his tea, buying time to choose his words carefully.

"I saw him go down," he said, squarely meeting Saleh's steely gaze. "We were in the midst of a firefight, and I had to deal with those still putting up resistance. By the time we'd taken care of the others, Karimi was gone."

"He disappeared?" Saleh scoffed. "Just like that?"

Faryad quickly intervened, eager to defuse the confrontation.

"I'm sure Karimi was well-trained, like all the Taliban," he told Saleh. "And no doubt had tried to slip into a hidden tunnel and make his escape, just as you did—though not as successfully."

Saleh knew Faryad had resorted to flattery in hopes of appeasing him. Much as it rankled him, the Taliban lieutenant played along, turning back to Rashid with what he hoped would pass for a look of conciliation.

"My apologies, General," he said. "It's just that Karimi could prove to be a loose cannon. I know the man personally—he was starting to have his suspicions about the way dissenters were being conveniently killed off in your attacks. If he's interrogated, he could tip our hand and undermine everything."

"From what my contacts at Bagram tell me, he's been unconscious since the Americans found him," Rashid assured Saleh. "He's not expected to survive surgery, much less be in any position to be questioned."

"If there's any chance he might survive, the risk is still there," Saleh countered. "And it's too great a risk to leave to chance."

"What are you suggesting?" Rashid said.

"The attack we'd planned on Bagram," Saleh said. "Though we've had to call it off, the teams are still in place. I say we make use of them."

The Taliban leader was referring to an intricate plan to attack the American military base during the U.S. President's scheduled visit to Kabul the following week. Just prior to meeting with the others, General Rashid had learned that the appearance had been canceled, and before they'd broached the matter of O'Brien's corpse and belongings, the three men had agreed to suspend the assault on Bagram. They still hoped for a chance to take out the President, but instead of carrying out the mission on their own, the men had decided it would be better instead to lend what resources they could to Kurdish militants from the PKK, whose operatives in Turkey were already targeting the Istanbul NATO conference, which the U.S. commander-in-chief still planned to attend. No contact had been made with the Turks yet, since those involved in the Bagram plot had yet to be diverted from the Afghan capital.

"I understand what you're suggesting," Faryad told Saleh, "but even if we could modify the plan and carry it out on short notice, would it really be worth it? Neutralizing a drone like Karimi hardly matches the importance of killing a president."

"I'm telling you," Saleh insisted, "if Karimi makes it through surgery and talks, it could set back everything we've been working for. Or worse."

Rashid, seeing a chance to smooth things over with Saleh, ventured, "The medical facility at Bagram would be an easy enough target. And security at the base won't be as heightened as it would have been for the President. We wouldn't need to stage a full assault."

The SVR agent mulled things over, then asked the Taliban leader, "How soon could you be in a position to carry this out?"

"My men could be ready at a moment's notice," Saleh said.

He turned to Rashid. "What about the men you have stationed on the base?"

"The same," the general responded. "Provided I can get through to them, they'd be ready to act within a matter of hours. Maybe sooner."

Faryad calmly finished his tea, then offered a whimsical smile. "This might well be a way to kill two birds with one stone. If we can silence Karimi while striking the Americans where it hurts, maybe it will give them extra incentive to get out of our way once and for all."

Saleh rose to his feet, signaling an end to the meeting. "Let's do it!"

6

Bagram Air Base, North of Kabul, Afghanistan

As he stepped off the bus that had brought him to the outskirts of Bagram Air Base, Nawid Pradhan couldn't remember the last time he'd felt this kind of hope. It was almost intoxicating. It reminded him of how he'd felt years ago, when he'd have friends over to his apartment for dinner and there would be wine, laughter, the squeals of playing children and spirited conversations that lasted long into the night. Perhaps, if all went well and Allah was willing, he would one day have that kind of life again. This day, he was certain, would be a step in that direction, a direction away from the despair and anguish that had dogged him since the Taliban had turned his world into ruin.

So high were the Afghan's spirits that, for once, he barely noticed how severely the threat of rain had increased the ever-present, gnawing ache in his arthritic hip. Yes, the pronounced limp was still there and Pradhan instinctively winced with each step, but he continued at a brisk pace along the dusty shoulder leading to the bazaar, oblivious to the dark clouds rolling in from the north.

The bazaar was a weekly affair. Just off the road a hundred yards from the entrance to the U.S.-NATO command center, more than a hundred local merchants and fledgling entrepreneurs were busily setting up shop at their usual locations.

Thunderstorms might have been forecast for later in the day, but no one seemed daunted as they went about their preparations. Some had erected sturdy booths inside well-secured tents, while others displayed goods set out on tables shaded by blankets propped on tall, rickety poles. Those with less means made do with arranging their wares on large rugs laid across the ground. There was a wide range of products: everything from small statues, holiday ornaments and bootleg DVDs, to freshly harvested produce, clothing and cigarettes. Most weeks Pradhan was among those looking to do business with soldiers from the base. His specialty was computer servicing, and there would always be at least a few officers looking to retrieve lost data or have their laptops tweaked so they would run faster.

This day, however, Pradhan had come to the bazaar not to sell, but to buy. Before boarding the bus back in Kabul, he'd received his meager weekly stipend from an Internet café where he worked a couple hours each day tending to computers. While a portion of the wages would go toward provisions to bring back to his family, he'd earmarked the lion's share for a new wardrobe. It wouldn't do to go to the interview wearing his normal tatters. It was important, he felt, to dress in a way that would make the best possible impression.

Pradhan took his time perusing several booths that featured slightly used Western clothing, finally settling on a pair of tan chinos, a white shirt and rattan sandals with expensive-looking tassels. The ensemble was more costly than he'd anticipated, but he felt it was money well spent. After all, what was a few hundred more afghanis? Once he got the job, it would only take him a day or two to make a return on his investment. And after a few months he would have made enough to afford a change of clothes for every day of the week. If he and his family continued to live frugally, by spring there would even be enough money to move into an apartment. Perhaps it would not be as nice as the one they'd lived in before their forced exile to Pakistan, but it would be a start and a welcome step up from living out of a cave.

Someone was using the makeshift changing tent behind the booth where Pradhan had bought his clothes. While he waited his turn, he bought a bottle of spring water, a bar of scented soap and a sponge so that he could clean away whatever grime he'd missed earlier while bathing in the icy waters of the Kabul River. He would be glad to put that ritual behind him. He'd been told at the job site that there was a shower in the employees' locker room—a shower with hot water, no less!

Once the changing tent was available, Pradhan went in and shed his old clothes, then hurriedly scrubbed himself from head to toe, anxious to rid himself of the telltale odor he knew would mark him as a transient. It was a laborious task, but he kept at it until his skin felt raw. Afterward, the Afghan hummed to himself as he tried on the new outfit. Everything fit perfectly, and when he eyed himself in a dusty mirror set in the corner, the one-time refugee beamed at his reflection, convinced he'd chosen well. Instead of a hapless vagrant, he looked like a working man, a man with a job and prospects for a better life. He flashed another smile, imagining the look on his wife's face once he presented himself to her later and gave her the good news. He hadn't yet told her about the job—he wanted it to be a surprise. After so many years of hardship and suffering, he looked forward to seeing, once again, a flicker of joy in her eyes. He longed, even more, to finally be able to tell her that her steadfast faith in him throughout all their sorrowful tribulations had not been in vain.

Once he'd adjusted the collar of his new shirt, Pradhan retrieved a neatly folded employment application form from the pocket of his old pants, then gathered up the rest of the clothes he'd changed out of and stared at them with disdain before tossing them into a waste container. Goodbye to the years of travail, he thought. As of this day, all that was behind him.

Pradhan was making his way out of the tent when he heard a commotion near the road. Several men were shouting angrily, and by the time Pradhan had circled around the clothing booth, the clamor had increased. A few dozen merchants had left their stations at the bazaar and were congregating around a convoy of three Army Humvees that had stopped alongside the road. A U.S. officer from the base had stepped out of the lead vehicle and was addressing the throng. Behind them, the soldiers in the other Humvees watched on warily, clutching M-16s.

"What's going on?" Pradhan asked a produce merchant who'd yet to leave his booth. The man's features were grim, tinged with anger.

"They've canceled the bazaar," he said.

Pradhan noticed the darkening horizon for the first time. "Because we might have a little rain?" he asked.

The merchant shook his head. Gesturing at the soldiers, he explained, "They say the base is in lockdown. No one's being allowed out or in."

Pradhan felt a sudden knotting in his stomach.

"Why?" he asked.

"Something about security," the other man replied skeptically. "As if we're about to attack them with bananas and CDs!"

"That's not a bad idea," a vendor in the next booth called out. "They say we'll be compensated for being 'inconvenienced.' Ha!"

Pradhan was disheartened by the news and as the shouting grew louder, he fought back his sudden anxiety. He hobbled away from the booths, making his way around the periphery of the angry mob.

"It doesn't mean the worst," he whispered to himself. Already, the words sounded hollow, though.

When he reached the road, Pradhan continued along the shoulder, heading toward the base. He hadn't gone far when one of the soldiers called out to him from the rear of a Humvee.

"Where are you going?"

The Afghan pretended not to hear and kept walking. His long, purposeful strides aggravated his hip, and with each step his limp became a little more pronounced. He tried his best to ignore the pain as well as the sound of the vehicle, which had shifted into gear and was backing up toward him.

"Sorry, sir, but the base is off-limits," the soldier called out to him as the vehicle drew closer.

Pradhan refused to acknowledge the soldier and trudged on, eyes straight ahead. The main gate was less than fifty yards away. He only made it a few steps farther, however, before the vehicle caught up with him and veered sharply onto the shoulder, blocking his way.

"You need to go back with the others," the soldier said. He was a young recruit, half Pradhan's age, pink-faced beneath his helmet. He was trying to be polite, but it was clear that he was issuing a command rather than a request, and though his carbine was aimed at the ground away from Pradhan, his finger was on the M-16's trigger.

"I have an interview!" Pradhan snapped, unable to rein in his frustration. "For a job at the base! Working on computers!"

"All job interviews have been canceled," the soldier told him. "There's been a temporary freeze put on hiring while we—"

"I have the job!" Pradhan insisted, waving his employment application. "Ask Mehrab Shah! He recommended me! The interview is just a formality!"

"I don't know anything about that, sir," the soldier replied. "All I can tell you is the situation has changed. No one is allowed to come onto the base without proper clearance."

"Ask Mehrab Shah!" Pradhan repeated. "He'll tell you! I have the job! I have clearance!"

"Have you gone through processing?" When Pradhan stared back, uncomprehending, the soldier rephrased the question. "Have they given you a background check?"

"I have nothing to hide!" he said.

"That's not what I asked, sir."

"I'm a loyal Afghan citizen who lost everything to the Taliban!" Pradhan shouted, his voice trembling with rage as much as desperation. "Four years I spent in the Pakistan refugee camps! Four years! I came back because there were promises we would have a chance to get something back! Empty promises! Now, finally, I have an opportunity!"

"I'm sorry, sir," the soldier said. "It's out of my hands."

"I'm begging you!" Pradhan pleaded. "This means everything to me!"

The soldier turned from the Afghan and glanced at the Humvee's driver, who offered only a faint shrug. A second recruit riding in the back of the vehicle shook his head with a look of resignation. The soldier looked back at Pradhan and was about to say something when he checked himself and instead reached for the walkie-talkie clipped to his belt.

"This Mehrab Shah," he said. "Whereabouts on the base does he work?"

"Mail and shipping," Pradhan said, tears welling in his eyes. "He does maintenance and deliveries. Please! You have to help me!"

The soldier keyed the walkie-talkie. As he raised it to his ear and waited for a response, he told the distraught Afghan, "Let me see what I can do."

AS HE RETURNED to his workstation following his nap break, Akira Tokaido shook his long wet hair, inadvertently flecking Aaron Kurtzman with a few wayward droplets.

"My dog used to do that," the cybercrew leader quipped.

"Sorry," Tokaido said. "I went up to the farmhouse to fix a computer after my nap, and thought I could beat the rain and took the grounds instead of the tunnel. Wrong choice."

"How bad is it out there?" Delahunt asked, glancing up from her computer as Tokaido plopped into his seat at the workstation next to her.

"I'm guessing we're in for at least another inch."

"Looks like Striker's in for a soaking, too," Kurtzman said, glancing at the BASIC sat-cam images he'd just called up on his computer. An unbroken mass of dark clouds stretched across Afghanistan all the way from Bagram Air Base to the Pakistan border. Any hope of catching a glimpse of Taliban movement in the mountain passes would have to wait.

As Tokaido started up his computer, he glanced over at Huntington Wethers.

"Your turn for a catnap, big guy."

Wethers shook his head without taking his eyes off his monitor.

"It'll have to wait," he said. "I'm in the middle of something."

"We all are, actually," Kurtzman added. He quickly briefed Tokaido on the latest developments in Afghanistan. Tokaido listened intently but was still able to split his focus and queue up the data windows he figured he'd need to put to use once he rejoined the cyber effort to lend Bolan assistance in the search for Howitzer O'Brien and the Taliban forces responsible for the recon officer's death.

"Last we heard, this Karimi fellow is out of surgery and should be up for questioning in a few hours," Kurtzman concluded. "Hopefully IE will be able to get him to spill." Kurtzman then turned from Tokaido to Wethers. "Any luck over there?"

"Not as much as I was hoping for," the African American said. He typed in a few more commands, then used his cursor to run another check with the Farm's Profiler search engine. The second-generation software program had security-cleared cross-links to the databases of more than five dozen law-enforcement entities ranging from metropolitan police forces on through the likes of Interpol, NATO Intelligence and the CIA. Wethers had entered ID photos of not only U.S. and NATO servicemen stationed at Bagram, but also all Afghan workers employed at the air base. The head shots had been cross matched with Profiler entries, not only in their original state, but also with computer-generated variants allowing for the chance that someone had grown facial hair, shaved his head or attempted thirty-one other ways of changing his appearance. Factoring in an earlier screening for discrepancies in personal data, Wethers had so far flagged, out of more than twenty thousand individuals, nearly three dozen persons of interest.

"None of them scream 'possible double-agent for the Taliban,'" he cautioned Kurtzman once he'd passed along his findings. "I've got soldiers with unreported misdemeanors, a couple officers with padded résumés and some workers with blanks on their job apps or multiple spellings for their last names, which can usually be chalked up to language snafus."

"I hear you," Kurtzman said. "Go ahead and set up a slide-show of the mug shots so we can see what we're working with."

While Wethers readied the presentation, Kurtzman leaned across his workstation and toggled an intercom, putting him in touch with Brognola and Price, who'd left the Computer Room earlier to confer with a blacksuit commander at the Security Operations Center.

"We're still tied up here," Brognola answered over the speakerphone once Kurtzman apprised him of Wethers's findings. "Go ahead and run through the pics, then see if you can prioritize the list before sending it along to Striker and Bagram AI."

"Gotcha."

Kurtzman clicked off, then shifted his wheelchair so he'd have a better view of the monitor on the far wall that Wethers had designated for running the mug shots.

"You heard the man," he told his colleague. "Let's roll it. Pause on each shot and let us know why the guy was flagged. We'll grade them on a 1 to 10 scale in terms of likely suspicion and take it from there."

"How about some popcorn while we're at it?" Delahunt said.

Kurtzman smiled wryly. "I don't think that made the cut with our union demands."

The cyberteam had been through this exercise before, and it took them less than ten minutes to scrutinize the mug shots. Of the thirty-one possible suspects, nineteen were U.S. soldiers, none of whom were given a higher rating than 3. Seven NATO soldiers were given an equally low priority. That left six Afghan workers. Four of them passed muster and were given ranks between 2 and 4. A fifth was bumped up to a 6 only because one of the Profiler's photo enhancements suggested that, given a beard and longer hair, the worker bore a passing resemblance to a convict who'd done time in Kabul for black marketeering handmade grenades.

The sixth of the flagged workers had been cited for the use of several aliases, one of which was linked to militia recruitment on behalf of one of the mujahideen warlords displaced from power after the current president of Afghanistan was elected to office. It was, at best, spurious grounds for suspicion, but given the relatively more benign infractions of the others, it was decided that the worker should top the list of those whom Bolan and Bagram's Army Intelligence should take a closer look at.

Of the worker's various aliases, Wethers designated the suspect by the name listed on his work permit—Mehrab Shah.

AS HE RODE THE FREIGHT elevator down from the second floor break room at the Bagram Parcel Station, Mehrab Shah was talking football with a couple U.S. recruits who worked in the main warehouse. Shah's English was easily the most fluent of any of the local Afghans working at the military base and this, coupled with his love for Hollywood movies and a ready knowledge of the American sports scene, had endeared him to the soldiers. Not surprisingly, he'd come to be not only well-liked but also trusted to the point where he was one of the few employees allowed to work with minimal supervision.

"The way they're playing, it will be New England in the Super Bowl," the thirty-year-old worker predicted. "I'll bet five dollars they win that, too."

"I'll take that bet, Shah-man," the older recruit told him once the elevator stopped and they moved out into the main corridor. "Chargers are gonna take it all."

Shah laughed. "You're either crazy or from San Diego."

"You think so?" The American grinned. "How about we make it ten bucks, then?"

"You're on, Mel-man." Shah turned to the other worker. "How about you? You want to lose some money, too?"

The younger recruit shrugged. "Sorry, man. I don't follow hockey."

Shah and Mel cracked up, then the Americans headed off for the mail room. Shah, meanwhile, went to retrieve his cleaning cart from an alcove under the nearby stairwell. Once his back was to the Americans, he dropped his smile and scowled to himself.

"Idiots," he muttered under his breath.

Shah had despised the United States even before he'd come to work at the base, but the more he'd studied their culture and ingratiated himself with the soldiers, the more he'd come to loathe their petty values and trivial concerns. Whether it was by jihad or some other means, Shah lived to see the day when America and its NATO allies would be put in their place once and for all. He yearned to assist in their downfall and had been looking forward to abetting in the assassination of their foolish President during his scheduled appearance at Bagram. This morning's news that the visit had been canceled had left the Afghan brooding inwardly, though he'd taken a perverse solace in the ease with which, once again, he'd duped the American recruits with a little small talk. It never ceased to amuse him how easily these gullible upstarts would drop their guard whenever he played the eager convert. Maybe the assassination had been called off, but Shah was confident there would be other opportunities, and when the time came for him to show his true face and deal a mortal blow against the heathens, he couldn't wait to see the dumbfounded look on their faces.

When he reached the end of the hallway, Shah used a key card to access the maintenance supply room. Once he'd wheeled his cart in, he closed the door behind him and made sure it was locked. He knew the routines of the janitors working the building. He had at least twenty minutes before anyone else came by for supplies, leaving him plenty of time to check in with his outside contacts.

Half the length of the right wall was taken up with personal lockers delegated to Shah and the other local workers. Next to the lockers a coffeemaker and condiment tray rested on a card table set against the wall. Shah donned a pair of snug-fitting latex cleaning gloves, then pulled out one of the folding chairs near the table and carried it to the opposite end of the lockers. He positioned it close to the wall, then stepped up onto the seat, putting himself within reach of the acoustic tile ceiling. The tiles rested on a framed gridwork, and when he nudged one of them, it gave way, tilting upward so that he could reach into a narrow cavity that housed sprinkler lines as well as conduits for the air-conditioning system. Rising on his tiptoes, Shah extended his hand until it closed around a small cell phone.

Shah, like all the other Afghan employees, was routinely searched before entering or leaving the base, and cell phones were just one item on a long list of contraband forbidden for security reasons. This particular phone had been smuggled onto the base for Shah's use by the man who planted him at Bagram as an agent for rogue forces within the Afghan National Army. When he flipped the cell phone open, Shah saw that he had a message. He accessed the call and heard a short series of tapping sounds that he knew had been made by the light drumming of a fingernail. It was a simple code instructing him to call back ASAP regarding a priority assignment.

Shah felt a twinge of anticipation as he hurriedly punched a phone number.

General Rashid picked up on the second ring.

"You called just in time," Rashid told Shah. "We have a situation for you to attend to at the medical center. How soon can you get there?"

"It's at the opposite end of the base, but I can be there in twenty minutes."

"I can give you thirty," the general replied, "but the plan is already in motion and you'll need to be ready to make your move at the top of the hour exactly. Is that clear?"

"Of course. Just tell me what needs to be done."

Shah listened carefully, plotting his next moves even as he committed Rashid's plan to memory. Much of it was a scaled-down version of the plot by which they'd hoped to kill the American President during his visit to Bagram, but in this case there was another target. And this time, rather than a mere facilitator, Shah would be the triggerman.

"Any questions?" Rashid said once the plan had been laid out in full.

"None," Shah replied. "I'm on my way."

The Afghan clicked off, then reached back into the cavity, returning the phone to its hiding place. Then groping farther into the recess, he retrieved a 10-round, silencer-equipped Walther P-22 pistol every bit as deadly as the expression on his face.

Shah raised the back of his work jacket and tucked the weapon in his waistband, then stepped down from the chair and brushed his footprints off the seat. He was putting the chair back when he heard someone trying to open the door to the supply room.

"You in there, Shah-man?"

It was Mel, the orderly Shah had exchanged bets with earlier.

Shah drew in a quick breath, composing himself.

"I'll be right there." Shah quickly removed the latex gloves and stuffed them in his pocket, then grabbed a pack of cigarettes from his cleaning cart. He lit one long enough to take a few quick puffs, then stubbed it out and waved his hand as if he were concerned about the smell of smoke. By the time he opened the door, he'd plastered his face with a sheepish grin. When Mel sniffed, Shah offered a contrite shrug.

"You caught me," he said.

"Jeez, Shah, can't you just do it outside?" Mel said. "You'll get your ass canned if you don't watch it."

"You're right," Shah said. "I was being stupid."

"Look," Mel went on, "somebody's calling from the front gate. Something about a guy coming by for a job interview. Name's Nawid, I think. He says you've greased the skids for him."

Shah did his best to look perplexed. He'd forgotten all about Pradhan, and the last thing he needed to deal with at the moment was cashing in a favor for one of his father's friends from the old days. Shah was already cutting it close in terms of getting to the medical center in time to carry out the plan. There was no way he was about to jeopardize things.

"I don't know anything about it," he lied.

"You sure?" Mel said. "Sounds like this guy mentioned you by name."

Shah shrugged. "It's happened before. You know how it is. Somebody gets your name and figures if they throw it around it'll get them somewhere."

"You wanna talk to the gate?"

Shah glanced at his watch and shook his head. "I still have deliveries to make, and I'm behind schedule."

"Sneaking an extra smoke break'll do that."

"So sue me," Shah joked. Then, more seriously, he added, "Can you just tell them I don't know the guy?"

"No prob," Mel said. "I was thinking, though… You want to up that Bowl bet to twenty bucks?"

Shah forced a grin. "Sure thing, Mel-man. Just make sure when you pay up, it's in afghanis. By January your American dollar will be worthless!"

Mel laughed. "We'll see about that!"

Shah waited for the orderly to head back to the mail room, then turned and briskly headed the other way. The shipping room was at the far end of the hall. When he reached it, he beelined to a long counter where recruits were waiting in line to pick up mail. At the end of the counter was a canvas gurney half-filled with parcels. Shah pointed to it as he waved to one of the postal clerks.

"I know I'm a little early," he said, "but it looks like there's a lot to be delivered."

"What else is new," the clerk said.

Shah inspected a couple of the top parcels, then told the clerk, "Anything for the medical center? I'll be right by there."

"Lemme check." The clerk scanned a stack of boxes that had just arrived by conveyor belt from the shipping warehouse. He brought two of them over to Shah. "Here you go. Good thinking."

Shah shrugged modestly. "Hey," he said, "just trying to help."

7

Nawid Pradhan was numb.

He'd managed only a few steps away from the soldiers in the Army vehicle before his legs had weakened beneath him, bringing him to his knees. The knot in his stomach had worked its way up into his chest and tightened. It was as if the oxygen was being blocked from his lungs. Pradhan felt dizzy as he stared blankly past the Humvee and the air base. Off in the surrounding mountains he could hear a distant rumble of thunder, and when a jagged streak of lightning pierced through the dark clouds, the Afghan native found himself wishing one of the bolts would strike him down and put him out of his misery once and for all.

He couldn't believe what had happened. Shah had denied knowing him? Denied that he had a job? Why? It made no sense. Shah knew how important this was. Pradhan wondered if he'd done something wrong. Had he disrespected the man somehow? Was he supposed to have paid him a bribe? It wasn't enough that he'd saved Shah's father's life the day the Taliban struck their apartment complex?

Pradhan's mind continued to spin, searching for answers. Over and over he gnawed at every detail of the last conversation he'd had with Shah in hopes he might find some clue to explain what had gone wrong. The obsession got him nowhere, and soon he was salting the wounds with self-recrimination over the money he'd squandered on clothes that were now little more than a blatant reminder of his blind hopes and foolish optimism.

Caught up in his grim ruminations, Pradhan was oblivious to the activity around him. Two ramshackle trucks had pulled to a stop near the bazaar, filled with townspeople from Kabul. They were already shouting angrily as they spilled out onto the road. Some carried crude placards scrawled with handwritten anthems. Though their cause had nothing to do with the cancellation of the bazaar, the merchants were quick to join their ranks, creating a large, teaming mob that advanced toward the gates leading to the air base. The three Army Humvees slowly eased backward as the soldiers on board shouted in vain for the crowd to turn back.

The spectacle had made its way past Pradhan when a burka-clad middle-aged woman broke away from the crowd and approached him, snapping him out of his reverie.

"How would you like to make a few afghanis?"

Pradhan wearily glanced up at the woman, who was holding out a cardboard sign taped to a flat wooden stick. He was still too disoriented to bother reading the message. He'd lost his will, as well, and when the woman placed the sign in his hand and helped him to his feet, he meekly went along and soon he was marching with the others toward the gate. Pradhan had no idea what was happening, but at this point it was of no consequence to him. Nothing mattered anymore.…

It had been nearly three years since a CIA-launched MQ-1 Predator had malfunctioned over the mountains just east of Kyber Pass, causing the unmanned drone to glide its way into a shallow lake less than a mile from the Pakistani tribal village it had intended to place under aerial surveillance. The drone, which had sustained minimal damage, had been retrieved by Taliban forces sequestered in the region. Over the next year-and-a-half, a crew of three technicians, including two renegade sympathizers from the Research and Development arm of Russia's Ministry of Defense, had painstakingly repaired not only the unmanned aircraft but also its AN/AAS-52 Multi-spectral Targeting System and the water-logged guidance systems of its two AGM-114 Hellfire antitank missiles. It had taken another fourteen months for the Taliban to procure enough components off the black market to cobble together a compatible ground control system. The reclamation project, from start to finish, had been overseen by SVR agent Eshaq Faryad, who'd subsequently earmarked the Predator as the key weapon in the planned assassination of the U.S. President during his visit to Bagram Air Base. That plan may have been scrapped, but the Predator was about to be put to use as a diversionary ploy in the effort to guarantee the silence of captured Taliban warrior Azzizhudin Karimi.

"The lightning is a concern, but if all goes well it will work to our advantage," Torialaye Yung reported. The goateed, scar-faced Uzbekistan technician who'd rounded out the crew that had salvaged the MQ-1 was on his cell phone, eyes on the black, swollen sky overhead as he spoke with Faryad from a remote mountaintop eleven miles north of Bagram. He was standing alongside the large truck that had been used to transport the disassembled drone to its launch site. The side of the truck had been stenciled with a logo for the Afghanistan Endangered Species Organization, which routinely patrolled this stretch of mountains to safeguard dwindling populations of markhors and snow leopards. The ruse had allowed Yung to access the restricted area without drawing suspicion, and now that the Predator had been removed from the truck, his two colleagues were deftly piecing the aircraft back together.

"How long before you launch?" Faryad inquired.

"Less than two minutes," Yung replied. "We'll use the cloud cover to get within firing range."

"There's no chance of an intercept?"

"As I said, the weather is in our favor," Yung answered. "Even if they manage to lock in, it will be too late to stop us."

"See it through, then, and report back," Faryad told his underling. "And when this is finished, there's another matter for you to attend to."

"What would that be?"

"We've gotten our hands on an enemy field computer," Faryad said. "I need your help to crack the access code."

Yung smiled to himself, then told Faryad, "I look forward to the challenge."

BOLAN HAD SPENT enough years in the field to know the value of rest. As sore as he'd been upon returning to Bagram after the debacle in Safed Koh, the moment he'd reached his assigned barracks after medical treatment, the Executioner had stretched out on an unused cot and closed his eyes, blocking out the pain as well as his concerns over how best to deal with the latest turn of events. Within moments he'd dropped into a deep and dreamless slumber, giving his body a chance to recover from the beating it had taken. He'd awakened six hours later, recovered enough to resume his mission. After a morning briefing with Army Intelligence, Bolan had reported back to Stony Man Farm, then he stopped by the medical center to have his shoulder stitches inspected and to change the dressing on several raw abrasions sustained during the previous night's mayhem. He'd also been outfitted with a two-layered ankle brace and a pair of calf-high combat boots to provide extra support.

Bolan had decided to test the ankle with a late-morning walk around the perimeter of Bagram's airfield. Each step brought a faint twinge, but he was secure on his feet and felt he'd be ready for whatever course of action the day would bring. He continued to hope things would play out in such a way that he could see to the recovery of O'Brien's body. For him, it was more than a mere matter of honoring a code of battle. There'd been a moment between O'Brien's rants about military strategy that the recon officer had mentioned his family back in the States, and Bolan knew that having a body to lay to rest would help his survivors find closure once they learned of his death. There, too, was a part of him that felt a kinship, however uncomfortable, with the man who'd so staunchly taken his government to task for what he saw as wayward policy. During that dark time when Bolan had stood in defiance of Washington, he'd been disillusioned at how readily his grievances had been dismissed. If they'd had their way, he would have been swept under the carpet like so much inconsequential dirt. He wasn't about to see O'Brien suffer that fate. Despite his disagreements, the man had still committed himself to fighting for his country and had paid the ultimate price. For that, he deserved whatever the Executioner could do to see that his final resting place would be on American soil.

Bagram had one lone runway, a wide, ten-thousand-foot-long asphalt ribbon stretching the entire length of the base. With lightning on the horizon there was minimal activity on the tarmac. Maintenance crews were at work on several fighter jets, and helicopters idled on offshoots linked to the runway. Bolan knew that once the storm passed, the aerial force would take to the skies, ready to carry out surveillance and, if the chance arose, engage the enemy.

Circling around a large, windowless storage bunker just off the runway, the Executioner suddenly found himself in the path of a small, fast-moving electric cart being driven by an Afghan local. Bolan lurched to one side as the man swerved and then braked, spilling a few parcels. Once the cart came to a stop, the Afghan bounded out to retrieve the packages.

"Sorry, boss," he told Bolan. "My bad."

"What's the hurry?" Bolan asked as he helped reload the cart.

"Everybody wants things delivered stat," the Afghan explained as he climbed back behind the wheel. "I tell them haste makes waste, but they still say 'Hurry.'"

The driver apologized again, then continued on. Bolan watched him speed past the storage shed toward a vast tract near the runway that had been cordoned off to serve as a salvage yard for totaled combat aircraft and ground vehicles. In addition to casualties from the U.S.-NATO arsenal, there were also rusting Afghan Su-series jets, as well as Soviet tanks and MiGs dating back to the Russian occupation. A pair of mechanics roamed about a recently grounded Black Hawk, dismantling usable components and loading them into two nearby pickup trucks. Helping with the chore were two young Afghans. When the delivery cart pulled up to them, the Afghans wandered over to speak to the driver.

Bolan had been assured earlier that Army Intelligence would be running a deeper security check on locals employed at the facility, but he had misgivings about Afghans having been hired in the first place, especially in light of what had happened the previous night. If the ambush attacks in the mountains had been triggered by information leaked from the base, Bolan felt it more likely the mole would turn out to be a civilian planted by the Taliban than some turncoat within the ranks of the military.

Bolan was still watching the exchange at the salvage yard when the wind shifted, carrying with it the sound of chants and shouting. The Executioner glanced to his left and traced the clamor to activity near the main entrance. A few dozen men and women had congregated before the concrete barriers that fortified the gates. Some waved placards while others raised fists as they directed taunts at the soldiers standing guard before them, both on foot and in several Humvees idling near the barricades. Elsewhere on the grounds, Bolan saw reinforcements emerge from nearby barracks and head toward the commotion, armed with M-16s.

"Protest rally," someone called out to Bolan. He turned and saw Rob Kitt striding toward him, one eye on the demonstration. The Infantry captain was unarmed but had on his boots and a fresh set of combat fatigues.

"Protesting what?"

"From what I hear, it started out when we canceled the bazaar on account of the lockdown," Kitt said. "Now it's more about wanting us gone."

"They really want a pullout?"

"Seems that way," Kitt said. "And this isn't the first time they've shown up. They've been by nearly every day the past couple weeks. Every time they come, the crowd's a little bigger."

"Strange way of showing gratitude," Bolan said.

"I'll second that," Kitt said. "I don't care what kind of a roll the ANA's been on. Without us, the government here would go under faster than you can say 'Taliban.'"

Bolan changed the subject. "So, what's AI doing in terms of the locals that work here?"

"That's what the lockdown's about," Kitt said. "Nobody else is coming in, and they're combing the grounds to question the guys still on duty. Anybody who gives off the wrong vibe gets taken aside for a more thorough interrogation. On top of that, they're going over all the personnel paperwork and looking for guys to run a deeper check on."

Bolan nodded approvingly. It seemed like the right course, and he felt certain that the latter task was being duplicated back in Virginia by Stony Man's cybercrew.

"We've got a couple breaks already on another front, though," Kitt said. "For starters, that Karimi guy they put under the knife is out of surgery and it looks like we'll be able to question him once the anesthesia wears off."

"Sounds promising," Bolan said. "What else?"

"IE just got the autopsy results on those bushwhackers we brought in. They might not be able to talk, but we hit pay dirt anyway."

"What'd they come up with?"

"Turns out most of 'em ate within an hour before they came after us," Kitt reported. "Big item on the menu was a fried wheat bread called mantou. It's a staple in China, but we know a few tribes in Pakistan that live off the stuff, too."

"Narrows things down a little."

"It gets better," Kitt explained. "Half the men were wearing boots lined with alpaca fleece. Apparently only one of the tribes breeds those suckers, and they're known for their boots. Add it all up and you gotta figure that's where this Taliban crew was being harbored."

"Where exactly are we talking about?" Bolan asked.

"Balqhat," Kitt said. "It's a small village in the hills just south of Parachinar."

It made sense. Parachinar, capital of Pakistan's Federally Administered Tribal Areas, was located a few miles downhill from the Safed Koh Range, at most a two-day hike from where the previous night's confrontations with U.S. troops had taken place. Bolan knew the area had long been known as a Taliban breeding ground and, according to most intel, Osama bin Laden and his minions had camped there while masterminding the 9/11 plane attacks in the U.S. How appropriate, Bolan thought, that destiny had pointed the way back to such a symbolic destination.

"Before you slap on your six-guns and go all Rambo, a word of caution," Kitt advised. "Cross the mountains and it's not just Taliban you'll have to deal with. Over there you've got not only tribal factions but also the Pakistan military thumping their chests and shouting 'sovereignty.' And unlike our little fan club over at the gate there, we're talking about an armed force ready to bite as much as they bark."

"I'll consider myself forewarned," Bolan said.

Kitt grinned. "But you're still going, aren't you?" When Bolan didn't respond, the captain said, "Well, you won't be alone."

Bolan was about to insist that he go solo when his PDA vibrated in his hip pocket. He excused himself and wandered off a few yards to field the call. It was Kurtzman, apprising him of the "suspect list" Wethers had coughed up with the help of SOG's Profiler.

"There's a file with mug shots in your e-box," Kurtzman told Bolan. "I sent it to AI, too, so you might want to touch base with them and divvy up the search."

"Will do," Bolan said. He quickly passed along the Balqhat lead, then signed off and switched over to his online screen. Within a few moments, he was viewing the slide show depicting those men on the base deemed worthy of greater scrutiny. When he came across the photo of Mehrab Shah, Bolan froze the screen.

Shah was the driver of the delivery cart that had nearly run him down.

Bolan logged off and stuffed the PDA back in his pocket as he glanced toward the salvage yard. The cart was nowhere to be seen, and one of the flatbed trucks had just pulled out of the yard and was heading toward a cluster of buildings located behind the air-base control tower.

"Problem?" Kitt asked.

Bolan nodded and gestured toward the salvage yard. "We need to check something out."

Bolan filled Kitt in as they strode briskly toward the yard. "I had him right in front of me," he finished.

"I wouldn't sweat it," Kitt countered. "Sounds to me like he's a long shot for being in on anything we need to worry about."

Bolan's gut instincts told him otherwise, and once the men passed through the gate leading to the scrapped aircraft, his worst fears were confirmed. The two Army mechanics he'd seen earlier lay sprawled in the dirt alongside the partially dismantled Black Hawk, and there was no sign of the Afghan laborers who'd been working alongside them.

Kitt followed as Bolan raced to the bodies. Both men had been gunned down at close range and blood seeped from head shots.

"What the hell," Kitt muttered. "I didn't hear any shots."

"Silencer," Bolan guessed.

Kitt noticed that the mechanics' holsters were empty. "Well, they've got a couple more guns on them now, too."

Bolan scanned the grounds just in time to see the missing truck round a corner and disappear amid the clustered structures behind the control tower.

"What are those buildings over there?" he asked Kitt.

"Fuel depot and administration offices," Kitt replied. "Doesn't seem like that's where they'd be headed, though."

Bolan stared past the buildings at another, larger structure—the one where he'd been treated for his battle injuries. Recalling Kitt's update on Karimi's pending availability for interrogation, he suddenly broke toward the truck that had been left behind. Kitt followed.

"You're right," Bolan told the captain. "They're headed for the med center."

8

With air traffic suspended, the control tower crew at Bagram Air Base was hard-pressed to stay on task. To the west, they had a clear view of the main gates and the chief flight controller found himself watching the confrontation between increasingly irate demonstrators and an ever-growing force of U.S. and NATO troops.

"This could get ugly real quick," he told the others.

One of the man's colleagues tracked down a pair of binoculars and peered through them, then shrugged. "Once they blow off some steam they'll peter out like they always do."

"I don't know about that," the controller said. "This is the first time they've started throwing things."

"It's just produce," the other officer said. "If they were lobbing grenades, it'd be another matter."

"Still, I hope there's some tear gas ready."

As he was lowering his binoculars, the other officer noticed activity closer to the tower. A flatbed truck had just rolled past, rounding the corner so wide it nearly clipped one of the fenceposts in front of the fuel depot. A few large pieces of scavenged equipment from the downed Black Hawk skidded noisily from one side of the truck bed to the other.

"Got a couple clowns out joyriding."

The controller eyed the swerving truck. "They probably want to get to the demonstration before it breaks up. If this storm hangs around, it might be the closest thing they see to action this week."

A third member of the tower crew, Signal Corps Officer Manny Ward, fought off the temptation to join the others and instead kept his attention focused on the radar screen. He was tracking the cloud movement, since once the storm passed, it would be on his say-so that the base would resume its aerial missions. So far, it looked as if the brunt of the anticipated downpour would hit the mountains and foothills or possibly veer north past the air base toward Charikar.

"Whoa!" he suddenly exclaimed, waving to the others without taking his eyes off the radar. "Come take a look at this!"

When the others joined him, Ward pointed to a slow-moving blip in the upper-left quadrant of the screen. Any concerns over the wayward truck or activity at the gate quickly fell by the wayside, replaced by a sense of urgency on the part of all three men.

"Too small for a plane," the controller said, grabbing a dispatch microphone from the console beside him. "Not enough zip for a missile, either, but I still don't like the looks of it."

"A drone maybe?" Ward suggested.

"If it is, it's not one of ours," the other officer said.

The controller patched through a quick call to the northern-gate security detail, which had at its disposal a pair of Buk-M1 tank-mounted antiaircraft missile launchers. Once he got through to the station's captain, he barked a quick command.

"Possible aerial intruder at 11:45!"

MEHRAB SHAH PULLED the electric delivery cart to a stop near a loading dock behind the medical center and bounded out, quickly grabbing a small parcel from the back. Two orderlies unloading a FedEx truck backed up to the dock. When Shah rushed past them up the nearby steps, one of them called out, "Where's the fire, Shah-man?"

Shah forced a grin and joked back, "If I don't get caught up on these deliveries, they're going to trade me to Kandahar for a player to be named later."

The Afghan maintained his easygoing smile as he passed an African-American security guard manning the rear entrance.

"Whaddup, homes?" Shah said, feigning a gangsta accent as he traded high fives with the guard, who was twenty dollars richer this week thanks to a deliberately poor bet the Afghan had made on the Lakers-Jazz game.

"You're crazy, man," the guard replied, shaking his head with bemusement.

Shah continued his easy banter with other employees as he made his way to the admissions desk near the elevators. They lapped it up, as did the desk receptionist, who blushed when Shah winked at her and called her "Sweetcakes."

"Got something stat for post-op," he told her, holding out the parcel, though not close enough for her to see that the shipment was actually designated for the basement laboratory.

"Okay," the woman said.

Shah winked again, then went to the elevators and pressed the up button. There was a clock mounted on the wall next to him. Shah let out a breath and dropped the smile. He was running out of time. According to the plan laid out to him by Faryad, all hell would break loose in less than thirty seconds.

"C'mon, c'mon," he muttered, stabbing the button again.

Before any of the elevators could arrive, the main doors to the med center opened, admitting three uniformed members of Army Intelligence. Two of them had unslung their M-16s.

"Mehrab Shah?"

Shah glanced at the men but said nothing.

"We need to have a word with you," the senior officer said. "If you'll come with us, please…"

Shah's Walther was still tucked back in his waistband, pressing against his spine, two bullets lighter after having been used on the mechanics at the salvage yard. There was no way he could reach for it without drawing fire—it might as well have been stuck back up in the ceiling cavity at Mail and Shipping.

Shah had been deliberating his next move when a massive explosion sounded outside the facility. The med center hadn't been the target, but it was close enough to the blast that the entire building trembled as if in the grips of an earthquake. Windows shattered and the three AI agents, like everyone else on the ground floor, were knocked off their feet.

Shah went down, too, but unlike the others, he'd been expecting the diversion and was the first to react. He scrambled upright and pulled out his Walther as he staggered past the elevators to the stairwell. Throwing the door open, he turned back and fired off five quick rounds. One shot flew wild but the other four struck the men who'd come for him. He wasn't about to stay put long enough to see if he'd killed them. He barged into the stairwell and headed up to the second floor, taking the steps two at a time. Outside, there were a pair of follow-up explosions, each one jolting the building again. Shah careened first off the railing, then the stairwell wall, but managed to stay afoot.

There was pandemonium on the second floor. Hospital personnel were sprawled down the entire length of the main hallway, still trying to regain their bearings. Two guards had made it back onto their feet but were clearly disoriented and no match for Shah. He gunned them down, one shot each, as he stalked down the hall. He was nearly out of rounds so helped himself to one of the guard's MP-7 submachine gun, then strode into the post-op recovery room where Karimi lay unconscious, swathed in bandages and hooked up to an EKG, IV drip lines and a respirator. Most of the equipment had overturned during the explosions, but the monitor continued to give off faint bleeps in time with the patient's lethargic pulse.

"You'd have saved us a lot of trouble if you'd died when you were supposed to," Shah murmured as he took aim with the Walther. He put the gun's final round through Karimi's forehead, obliterating flesh, bone and brains. The monitor's steady bleep gave way to a high-pitched, uninterrupted drone. Karimi had flatlined. He would take to his grave any suspicions about Aden Saleh's collusion with General Rashid.

Shah then heard activity out in the hallway. He cast aside the Walther and swung the MP-7 into firing position. When the guard he'd exchanged high fives with earlier appeared in the doorway, Shah ignored the man's bewildered expression and calmly unleashed two rounds, killing him instantly.

No one else showed themselves, but Shah knew that would change soon enough. He kept the gun aimed toward the hallway as he backed around Karimi's bed and made his way to the window. The glass had already shattered inward, saving him the effort of breaking it. So far the plan had gone off almost without a hitch, and when Shah leaned out the window and saw his colleagues pulling up in the flatbed truck they'd commandeered from the salvage yard, he believed they had a good chance to not only carry out their mission, but to live to tell the tale.

BOLAN HAD JUST DRIVEN past the control tower when the Predator's Hellfire missile slammed into the Bagram fuel depot. Shock waves from the resulting explosion flipped the truck on its side, throwing Kitt clear while trapping the Executioner inside. Bolan had struck his head on the door frame and was momentarily dazed, but he shook it off and was pulling himself from the wreckage when spreading flames ignited two more fuel tanks in quick succession. The concussive force jostled the truck further and Bolan barely managed to scramble free before the flatbed flipped again, coming to a rest upside down, just inches from where Bolan had landed.

It wasn't over yet. As he slowly rose to his feet and glanced over the top of the upended truck, he saw a fireball erupt from the ruins of the fuel depot and sweep across the grounds toward him. There was no time for evasive action. Bolan threw himself back to the ground, face to the dirt, and clasped his hands behind his head, shielding his temples with his biceps.

The fireball had struck the truck squarely in the undercarriage. Flames engulfed the ruptured gas tank, triggering yet another blast. Instead of feeding the fireball, however, the explosion neutralized it. Bolan was spared from incineration but still had to contend with a shower of blazing shrapnel as one of the shards ignited his fatigues. The Executioner rolled through the dirt until the flames were smothered.

Surrounded by small, scattered fires, Bolan carefully rose to his feet. Thirty yards away, Kitt was clutching his shoulder but seemed otherwise unharmed. Others had not fared as well. Along with the stench of burning fuel, Bolan could smell the charred flesh of several smoldering, mangled soldiers lying in unnatural positions amid the debris of the flattened fuel depot. Nearby, the control tower had collapsed on itself. Two servicemen had fallen to their deaths and lay out in the open, while the third member of the crew was only partially visible, buried beneath the splintered remains of the control room.

Far off in the distance a tendril of lightning ripped through the dark clouds, drawing Bolan's gaze skyward just in time to see yet another explosion, this one high in the air less than a quarter mile from the air base. Kitt saw it, too, and as he watched bits of flaming debris trail down to the desert floor below, he called out, "When did they get drones?"

Before Bolan could respond, a pained cry sounded from the downed control tower. The officer trapped beneath the collapsed structure was still alive, weakly flailing one arm in hopes of drawing attention.

"I'll get him," Kitt told Bolan. "Go see what's happening at the med center!"

Bolan spotted an M-16 lying a few yards from one of the charred bodies near the fuel depot. The weapon had been scorched by the fireball and was still warm when the Executioner picked it up. He aimed it at the dirt and thumbed the safety, then pulled the trigger. It wouldn't fire. Bolan pitched it aside and sprinted toward the larger building. His sprained ankle was holding up, but his skull throbbed where he'd struck the truck's door frame, and he could tell that he'd sustained burns where his fatigues had caught fire. He knew it could have been a lot worse.

The medical center was still standing. Many of the employees had evacuated and were standing out front, murmuring to one another. There was no sign of either the electric cart or the other flatbed truck, so Bolan veered wide of the crowd and headed for the narrow driveway leading to the rear of the building. He entered the alleyway just in time to see Shah leap from the second story into the rear bed of the truck being driven by one of the Afghans Bolan had seen at the scrap yard. When the driver spotted the Executioner, he jammed the truck into gear and sped forward.

The alley was tight, flanked on one side by the hospital and on the other by a tall cinder-block wall. There was barely room enough for the truck, and Bolan had no place to dodge the oncoming vehicle. He wasn't about to turn his back, however. Undaunted, he stood his ground and let the truck bear down on him. As if two tons of rolling steel didn't seem likely enough to send the Executioner to his Maker, Shah had risen to his feet in the rear of the truck and was taking aim with his MP-7. He had Bolan dead in his sights. All he had to do was pull the trigger.

9

As the truck bore down on him, the Executioner dropped to a crouch, placing himself beyond range of the deadly steel penetrator rounds Shah had hoped would bring swift, certain death. Bolan's maneuver hadn't been strictly defensive. At the last possible second, he sprang forward and upward, torquing his body to one side, legs bent, so that he was facing away from the truck. The leap carried him above the truck's front end and sent him bounding across the hood. Bolan tucked in his chin and clasped his hands behind his head. When his momentum threw him against the truck's windshield, his back absorbed the blow while causing the glass to spiderweb and collapse slightly inward.

The truck had picked up enough speed to send Bolan up and across the roof. Before Shah could get off another volley, his intended target crashed into him and both men tumbled onto the truck bed, glancing off a section of fuselage from the scavenged Black Hawk. The rear tailgate was up and prevented the men from rolling out as the truck cleared the alley and sped past the front of the medical center, scattering evacuees. Veering around the fiery remains of the fuel depot, the getaway vehicle barreled down the road leading to the main gate.

The MP-7 had been knocked from Shah's grip. Both he and Bolan battled each other trying to reach the weapon first. Both still reeling from their collision, their initial blows were weak and tentative, but as they slowly recovered their ferocity increased. Bolan took an elbow to the jaw and knee to the thigh as he clipped the other man's skull with a karate chop that was too far off the mark to knock Shah out. The Afghan countered with a glancing head butt and drove his fist into Bolan's midsection. The Executioner grimaced but continued his own assault, ramming his left forearm against the other man's shoulder, following up with a cramped right cross that nailed Shah's chin. With a little more leverage, it might have been a telling blow, but even though the Afghan's head snapped back momentarily, he remained conscious and summoned enough strength to push away and reach for the submachine gun. He was closing his fingers around the stock when Bolan intervened, grabbed Shah's elbow and jerked his arm away. The MP-7 slid across the bed, wedging itself under the scrapped fuselage.

The stalemate continued as the truck gained speed, closing in on the main gate. Hoping to tip the scales, the Afghan riding shotgun in front of the truck decided to enter the fray. He used the butt of his stolen M-9 automatic to smash the cab's rear window, then pointed the gun through the opening, trying to get a clear shot at Bolan. The Executioner was a step ahead, however. He rolled to one side and grabbed Shah by his shirt collar, pulling him close and making him a human shield. In the same motion, he twisted his wrist, tightening the collar around Shah's neck. The Afghan gasped, choking, as he grasped at Bolan's hand.

It was the break Bolan had been looking for. He closed his free hand into a fist and swung backhanded as hard as he could, striking Shah in the jaw. Shah blacked out and collapsed on top of Bolan. The Executioner drew in his legs then kicked upward, catapulting his adversary away from him. The Afghan flew backward toward the truck cab, continuing to block his enemy's aim.

Bolan had bought himself a few precious seconds and he made the best of them, reaching across the truck bed for the nearest piece of salvage, a computer motherboard taken from the Black Hawk's cockpit. He tossed it like a Frisbee, missing the gunman's weapon but tearing a gash in his forehead. The gunman howled and reached for his brow, trying to stop the blood from flowing into his eyes.

The Executioner took advantage of the gunman's distraction and crawled past Shah, finally getting his hands on the MP-7. He drew it into firing position and burped two rounds into the man he'd just wounded. Blood filled the truck cab and sprayed the windshield, further obscuring the driver's visibility. When the gunman slumped into the driver, the truck began to swerve wildly, throwing Bolan to one side.

Shah, meanwhile, had regained consciousness. He grabbed the Executioner's arm, but Bolan quickly shook himself free and rammed the butt of the pistol against the other man's skull, knocking him out once again.

Lurching to his feet, Bolan grabbed the side of the truck to keep his balance. They were now less than twenty yards from the main gate. Up ahead, soldiers were scrambling to get out of the truck's path. The driver might not have been able to clearly see where he was going, but he'd floored the accelerator nonetheless, turning the vehicle into a rolling death trap.

Just as the truck was about to plow through the lowered wooden span blocking the main entrance, Bolan went over the side. He landed hard and tumbled across the asphalt as the truck shattered the plank and veered to the right, slamming into one of the concrete barricades with so much force it somersaulted, flinging Shah and the salvaged Black Hawk parts into the mob of demonstrators. There were screams as several of the protestors were struck down, and soon there was chaos on the roadway.

Back near the gate, a soldier approached Bolan just as he got to his feet.

"What the hell's going on?" he asked.

Bolan was in no mood for explanations. He broke away and staggered over to the MP-7 he'd dropped when jumping from the truck.

"We can't let them get away," the Executioner said.

"Take it easy, man," the soldier told him. "They aren't going anywhere."

Bolan willed himself to keep moving. He circled around the half-crushed barricade and advanced on the mob, which had tightened its ranks, even as a few of them retreated back toward the bazaar.

"There were three men in the truck!" Bolan shouted to the soldiers still poised in the nearby Humvees. "They need to be accounted for!"

THERE HAD BEEN A POINT during the demonstration when Pradhan had lost himself in the moment. Even though he had nothing against the Americans, he'd vigorously waved the sign given to him and for a time he'd even shouted its message— *"U.S./NATO must go!"* But as the din had increased and his voice had been drowned out, he'd amended his cry to one more personal—"Why did you betray me, Mehrab! Why did you turn your back on me!" Over and over he'd wailed his lament, at the same time allowing himself to get caught up in the escalating foment. What did it matter if he didn't share the others' viewpoint. It had been enough that they, like him, were fed up with their circumstances, and to take part in the shouting and gesticulating felt cathartic.

It wasn't until the merchants began taking their wares from the bazaar and throwing them toward the gate that Pradhan had finally given pause. It took him back to the first days of the Soviet invasion, all those years ago, when rock-flinging mobs had met with rifle fire and tank blasts. Even as those horrific memories were coming back to him, a series of resounding explosions had rocked the base. The merchants had been stunned, and even the demonstrators who'd arrived in the trucks had quickly sobered. Seized by a sudden sense of apprehension, Pradhan had dropped his sign and attempted to extricate himself from the demonstration. It was no use, however. He was in the thick of things, surrounded on all sides with no one willing to let him by. And so he'd remained, consumed with dread, watching black smoke billow ominously from the air base and wondering, like most of the others, what had happened.

It had gone on like this for minutes, the crowd at a standstill, their shouts replaced by uncertain murmurings. Then a truck had barreled down the road leading from the base, and the next thing Pradhan knew there had been a sickening crash and renewed cries as several large objects had rained down on the crowd.

And now it was all madness.

People moved in all directions, and in their haste they'd knocked Pradhan to the ground, soiling the knees of his new pants. It was all he could do to avoid being trampled as he struggled back to his feet. Beyond the fringe of the crowd, soldiers were firing in the air and demanding that everyone stay put, but no one paid attention. Pradhan disobeyed the command as well and began hobbling back toward the bazaar.

No more trouble, he thought to himself. I don't want any more trouble.

"Out of our way!" shouted someone, coming up on Pradhan.

Before he could react, the Kabul native was brusquely shoved to one side by one of four demonstrators carrying something between them. It was a man, visibly bruised and clearly unconscious. Pradhan initially thought it was somebody who'd been struck by the debris thrown from the overturned truck, but when he looked closer, he shuddered, incredulous.

They were carrying Mehrab Shah.

"Mehrab!" Pradhan shouted.

He limped alongside the four men, struggling to keep up. One of them warned him to stay away, but Pradhan continued to doggedly follow on their heels. Finally, one of the men let go of Shah and broke away from the group, pulling a hand-gun from beneath the folds of his clothing. He lashed out at Pradhan, pistol-whipping him to the ground.

"You saw nothing!" the man shouted.

When Pradhan stared up at him, bleeding from his right cheek, the man kicked him fiercely in the ribs, causing him to double over in agony.

"You saw nothing!" Pradhan's tormentor repeated.

The Afghan remained on the ground this time, fresh tears streaking his cheeks. The crowd around him had thinned out, and others rushing past took care not to run him down. Finally he sat back up, just in time to see a foglike cloud drifting toward him. His eyes began to burn and he felt his throat constrict as the mist settled over him.

Tear gas.

Moments later, several soldiers wandered into view, wearing gas masks and brandishing assault rifles.

"There's one more of them here somewhere!" one of the men shouted through his mask at those standing in his path. "Where is he?"

No one responded. Like Pradhan, everyone had been overcome by the gas, their chants and taunts replaced by a ragged chorus of coughing and retching. When the soldier reached him, Pradhan looked up, terrified. The gas mask gave the soldier the appearance of some large, malevolent insect.

"A man was thrown from the truck!" the soldier told him. "Where is he?"

Pradhan shrugged helplessly, rubbing the blood from his bruised face.

"I saw nothing," he gasped hoarsely. "I saw nothing."

WHILE SECURING A GAS MASK from one of the Humvees, Bolan had overheard an officer receiving confirmation that Azzizhudin Karimi had been shot to death back at the medical center. The news redoubled Bolan's resolve to find the man's killer. None of his most recent injuries were disabling, but the cumulative effect was pronounced and as he resumed the search each step was an ordeal. All around him, troops were scattering the crowd, breaking up any tight groups that might have been concealing the missing assassin.

"He was in no shape to get away on foot," Bolan told Master Warrant Officer Dennis Spiers, head of the main gate security detail.

"I'll buy that," Spiers called out through his mask as they made their way toward the bazaar. "The way he went flying out of that truck, most likely the bastard broke his neck."

"I'll believe it when I see it." Glancing down the road, Bolan added, "We need to get somebody after those trucks."

"Already on it," Spiers responded.

By the time the men reached the bazaar and began to search the various tents and booths, one of the Humvees from the main gate was racing past, hot in pursuit of the two vehicles that had brought the demonstrators to the site. The trucks had a mile lead and had just dropped from view into the first of several large, arid valleys that lay between the air base and Kabul. Moments later, an Apache gunship droned past, flying low over the ground to lend aerial support.

"What I don't get is why they pulled out all the stops," Spiers muttered as he surveyed a produce stand that had been picked clean once the demonstrators had begun pelting the servicemen. "Hell, this Shah fucker could've just slipped up to post-op and offed Karimi without all the fireworks."

"Maybe, maybe not," Bolan countered. "And if he'd acted alone, he'd have never made it off the base."

"Good point."

"The real question is who else was in on it," Bolan said. "No way was this just the Taliban. They had to have had inside help, and I don't mean just Shah and the guys on salvage duty."

Spiers nodded. "AI's got their work cut out for them."

The tear gas had dissipated by the time the two men had finished searching the bazaar. Bolan yanked off his mask, struggling to rein in his frustration.

"We'll need to detain these people for questioning," he told Spiers. "This whole demonstration was nothing more than a diversion."

"You're probably right," Spiers said. "I'll get on it."

The officer was grabbing his walkie-talkie when there was an explosion down the road, just past the incline.

"What now!" Spiers exclaimed.

The Executioner was already in motion. Looking for immediate transportation, Bolan noted a handful of vehicles parked next to the bazaar, and one of the merchants was loading the last of his goods into a dilapidated panel truck. The engine was idling and the merchant's teenage son was at the wheel. Bolan yanked the door open and gestured for the youth to get out. The boy stared down at Bolan's M-16, then glanced past him at Spiers, who was just a few steps behind.

"We need to borrow the truck," Spiers said. He spoke in Dari, raising his voice so that the boy's father could hear him, as well. The merchant nodded to his son, and the boy slid out from behind the driver's seat. Spiers moved past Bolan and climbed aboard.

"Go ahead and ride shotgun," he told the Executioner. "I've got experience driving these jalopies."

Bolan circled the vehicle and got in the other side. Spiers backed out onto the road, then put the truck in Drive and rumbled off. The men rode silently, neither wanting to voice their suspicions that matters had just taken another dark turn.

10

For the men in the Humvee pursuing those who had just fled the aborted demonstration, everything happened too quickly once they reached the incline leading away from the air base. The moment the road dipped, the driver was forced to slam on his brakes to avoid crashing into a small herd of goats meandering across the asphalt. The vehicle screeched to a halt less than a few yards shy of the creatures as well as a burka-clad woman who stood in the middle of the road, shepherding the beasts with a large cane. She glared at the soldier with what he at first mistook for anger at his reckless driving. When she cast the cane aside and reached inside the folds of her burka, however, he realized the woman's hatred ran far deeper.

"Bomber!" he shouted to the other men.

Before anyone could react, the woman lunged at the Humvee and threw herself on the front hood. The explosives strapped to her chest detonated, killing her and the driver instantly. The other two soldiers were thrown from the vehicle, maimed by shrapnel. They landed near the goats, half of which had been killed, as well. The others bleated wildly as they scampered off in all directions.

Thick clots of brush grew alongside the right side of the road, and moments later two men emerged from the vegetation carrying AK-47s. They ignored the fleeing goats and calmly strode toward the surviving soldiers, who lay writhing on the road amid flaming sections of the Humvee. Taking careful aim, they fired their rifles into the wounded men until they stopped moving.

Farther down the road, the two getaway trucks had reached the valley floor and were passing over a bridge that spanned a wide river fed by the snowcapped mountains to the north. The gunmen were glad to have played their part in facilitating the vehicles' escape, but there was no time to indulge in self-congratulation. Above the goats' howling and the crackle of flames emanating from the bombed Humvee, they could hear the approach of a helicopter. Both men dropped to a crouch and raised their Kalashnikovs skyward. It was unlikely their bullets would be any match for an enemy gunship, but they weren't the only insurgents to have bailed out of the trucks to lie in wait for pursuers. Off in the nearby shrubs, an older man had just propped a Soviet-made RPG-7V on his shoulder. Peering through the scope, he waited for the chopper to show itself so that he could fire the launcher's 40 mm warhead.

THE PANEL TRUCK REACHED the valley's rim ahead of the Apache.

Alerted by smoke trailing up from the road ahead, Spiers had slowed and turned onto the shoulder, positioning the vehicle perpendicular to the traffic lane he'd just abandoned. Bolan was on the valley side of the truck, and by the time it came to a stop he had a clear view downhill. He saw the burning Humvee as well as the casualties and the two gunmen. He was drawing bead on the latter with his M-16 when, out of the corner of his eye, he detected movement in the nearby brush. Shifting aim, he spotted a third man crouched behind the shrubs, a rocket launcher pointed past the panel truck at the sky. Bolan heard the Apache pass directly above him and knew the aircraft was going to be attacked. He wasn't about to let it happen.

The Executioner quickly switched the carbine to its single-fire mode and pulled the trigger. The increased accuracy paid off. He missed the rocketeer's head, but slammed his round into the man's shoulder just below where the launcher was propped. The man went down before getting his shot off.

Alerted by Bolan's report, the other two ambushers whirled and fired at the panel truck, punching holes in its side. Since Spiers had already bailed from the vehicle, Bolan slid across the bench seat and rolled out the driver's side. He dropped to a crouch next to the warrant officer as more rounds thumped against the vehicle.

"Party never stops around here," Spiers said.

The skirmish was taken over by the Apache. Its M-230 Chain Gun made quick work of the enemy, taking out the Kalashnikov team with its first salvo and then finishing off the man in the bushes before he could bring his rocket launcher back into play. When a sweep of the surrounding terrain failed to turn up any additional combatants, the gunship banked and drifted back to the valley rim long enough for the gunner to flash a thumbs-up to Bolan and Spiers. By the time the ground duo had gotten back inside the panel truck, the Apache was making its way downhill toward the retreating trucks.

"Keep an eye open," Spiers advised Bolan as he pulled back onto the road. "As much planning as they've put into this, it wouldn't surprise me if there's still more of 'em out there."

"Agreed."

Spiers drove carefully around the carnage on the road ahead, then slowly picked up speed. They reached the valley floor without further incident, and by the time they'd crossed the river, the Apache had overtaken the two trucks. Once the road reached a stretch running between a pair of steep, craggy hillocks, the gunship sped ahead, then swung about and slowly set down, barricading the road. The Chain Gun rattled anew, shredding the front tires of the lead truck and perforating its front grille with enough shots to put the engine out of commission. The truck rolled to a stop, as did the slightly larger vehicle behind it.

As Bolan and Spiers raced to catch up, the rear tailgates of both trucks dropped and those riding in back climbed out. Only a few of them were armed, and when they tried to take on the Apache, they were swiftly cut down by the M-230.

When the others attempted to retreat into the surrounding hills, the pilot bounded out of the chopper and fired warning shots over their heads with an M-9 pistol. As soon as Spiers pulled to a stop thirty yards behind the trapped trucks, Bolan backed the pilot up, peppering the hills with bursts from his M-16. Spiers quickly followed his lead. Realizing there was little chance of escape, the demonstrators, one by one, threw up their hands in surrender. As soon as the Apache's copilot disembarked, Bolan and Spiers left the roundup to the chopper crew and turned their attention to the two trucks.

"I'll take the one in front," Bolan said.

The Executioner approached the vehicle cautiously. A canvas flap had fallen back in place over the opening to the truck bed, blocking his view of whatever lay beyond it. When he was close enough, he crouched below the tailgate and raised his assault rifle, using it to jostle the flap. He waited a moment. Getting no response, he rose slightly and quickly yanked the flap to one side, ready to fire. It wouldn't be necessary. The truck was empty.

"Zip on this one," Spiers called out as he approached from the rear truck. "Any luck here?"

"Negative."

"Okay, I give up," Spiers murmured. "Where the hell is that bastard?"

BACK DOWN THE ROAD from where the fleeing demonstrators had been brought to a halt, two men eased a small fishing boat into the current of the river just beneath the bridge where they had waited patiently for the right opportunity to make their move. Inside the boat was an elderly shepherd dressed in rags, seated just in front of a piled heap of fresh-shorn wool clipped from the sheep he raised on a small farm located two miles up the river.

"Allah be with you," the other two men called out as the shepherd took up his oars and began to row.

"He's always with me," the shepherd called back.

For a person in his seventies, the old man was in good shape, with a strong back and even stronger arms. He plied his boat swiftly downriver, guiding it around raised boulders and equally large rocks lying just below the surface. He'd just navigated his way around a sweeping bend when he noticed a stirring amid the wool. A hand emerged, clearing away enough fleece so that the man lying beneath it could peer out from his place of hiding.

Mehrab Shah tried to speak but found that he couldn't. More than that, he was unable to close his mouth. His jaw was numb and swollen, and when he weakly ran his hand from one side of the chin to the other, he could feel a pronounced misalignment. The jaw was clearly dislocated.

The shepherd misinterpreted the disconcerted look on Shah's face and assured him, "We're almost there. Stay put."

Shah obeyed. His entire body ached and a searing pain pulsated through his skull. He was alive, though, and he consoled himself with the notion that he would be around to hear others tell of his heroics. Yes, martyrdom was glorious, but he preferred the alternative.

Several minutes later, the shepherd guided his boat toward a boulder-strewn embankment overrun with wild kudzu and shaded by a stand of ancient oak trees. The current tapered off, and the water was soon shallow enough that the shepherd was able to climb out and wade to shore, dragging the boat with him.

"It will take a moment to clear the opening," he told Shah.

Shah nodded. He was exhausted, and as he listened to the shepherd wrestling through the kudzu he allowed himself to drift off into unconsciousness, welcoming a respite from the pain. He came to moments later, feeling no better. Grimacing, he parted the layers of fleece and slowly sat up. After drawing in a few deep breaths, he summoned the strength to roll over the side of the boat. The river was cold but invigorating. He dropped to his knees and splashed his face with water, wincing when he inadvertently tapped his jaw.

Standing, he made his way ashore just as the shepherd was rolling aside a large boulder concealing the opening to a tunnel—a tunnel that, just like the one into which Aden Saleh had fled the previous night high up in the Safed Koh Range, had managed to avoid detection by U.S. and NATO forces during all the years they had been stationed in Afghanistan. Also like that other tunnel, this passage wound its way westward, where, eventually, it would link up shafts that would take Shah into the mountains bordering the safe haven of Pakistan.

"I was told you would be picked up here shortly," the shepherd told Shah. "No one will be able to find you before they arrive, so you might want to rest and gain your strength."

Shah was still unable to speak so he made do with a nod and entered the tunnel.

The shepherd bade Shah farewell, then stepped back and slowly eased the boulder back into place. He looked around and rearranged some of the kudzu to better conceal the rock, then made his way back to his boat. Minutes later, he was once more in the middle of the river, bound for Kabul, where, if he was lucky, his wool would fetch him a fraction of the money he'd just earned for aiding in Shah's escape.

By the time the shepherd had rowed a mile farther downriver, the Apache helicopter flew low overhead and began to track his course. The old man suspected that at some point he would be intercepted and searched. The prospect didn't concern him. They would find nothing in the boat, and if they questioned him, it would be in vain, because that would be all he'd give them. Nothing.

11

Spin Range, Nangarhar Province, Afghanistan

"It was a high price to pay to silence someone who might not have been able to give any information to the enemy," Torialaye Yung said to Eshaq Faryad. The two Uzbekistans stood outside the remote farm hut where Faryad had conspired with ANA General Rashid and Taliban leader Aden Saleh to arrange for the execution of Azzizhudin Karimi.

"It had to be done," Faryad assured his comrade. "But, yes, I wish it hadn't cost us the Predator, especially after all the time you put into making it operational."

"It cost us the ground control system, as well."

After sending the drone to attack Bagram Air Base, Yung and his Russian counterparts had driven the truck containing the GCS to a mountain lake three miles downhill from the launch site. There, they'd put the truck in gear and then scrambled clear, allowing the vehicle to roll forward and plunge over the side of a cliff into the mile-deep water. With it went the monitoring equipment that Yung had used to guide the MQ-1 to its target, thereby unleashing the Hellfire missile that had destroyed the base's fuel depot. The men had earlier left a nondescript sedan parked near the lake, and after driving to Raqi, Yung had dropped off his colleagues at a Taliban safe house and proceeded alone toward the Pakistan border. Abandoning the main highway a few miles south of Jalalabad, he used side roads to reach the remote enclave where he now stood with Faryad.

Downhill from the hut, laborers were busy sowing a vast field with poppy seedlings. By spring the plants would be ready to be harvested for opium and processed into heroin. As he and Yung watched the planting, Faryad reflected, "If we have a good crop, we'll be able to replace the Predator and then some."

"Provided we can find one on the black market," Yung said.

"We'll see when the time comes."

"You mentioned getting your hands on a field computer," Yung said, anxious to put the Predator's loss behind him and move on.

"It's inside," Faryad said. "Before you start with that, come and let me show you how we dispose of the soldier it belonged to."

Yung shrugged and followed Faryad past the heap of melting snow where O'Brien's body had been set previously and then up a trail that wound through several tall stands of holly trees. As they walked, Faryad filled in Yung on the aftermath of the Predator attack on Bagram, concluding with word that Shah had eluded capture and was reportedly bound for the mountain compound.

"We've sent medics to meet him in the tunnels," Faryad said. "He's not in the best of shape, and we'll probably need to get him to a hospital once he's brought here."

"I know Mehrab," Yung said. "I'm not surprised he survived."

"Allah protects those we can make the best use of."

Yung chuckled. "I guess that would explain how I made it here without incident."

Once the men cleared the holly, they found themselves standing before a small, abandoned marble quarry surrounded by a high, barbed-wire fence. Saleh stood just inside an opened gateway near the edge of the pit. Next to him a crude wheelbarrow held O'Brien's bluing corpse. General Rashid paced a few yards away, back turned to the Taliban leader, conversing on his cell phone.

Saleh greeted Yung, then told him, "You're just in time. The food's starting to spoil."

The technician looked confused.

"I didn't explain everything," Faryad told Saleh with a faint smile.

Saleh chuckled, then glanced over his shoulder and stared into the pit a moment before circling to take hold of the wheelbarrow.

Faryad and Yung moved closer as Saleh rolled O'Brien's body to the brink, then tipped the wheelbarrow, dumping the slain officer's body into the pit. It was a twenty-foot drop to the quarry floor, and the men could hear the brute force with which the corpse landed. The noise also drew the attention of the pit's occupants.

Four fully mature snow leopards soon emerged from their darkened lair and padded toward the body, which lay amid a sprawl of bones and animal skulls picked clear during previous feedings.

"Their usual diet is live goats," Saleh said, "but I'm sure they won't mind a change to the menu."

Yung watched on with morbid fascination as the leopards sniffed O'Brien's corpse, then began to tear at it. The largest of the beasts was quick to rip loose one of the captain's arms and trot off to one side, leaving the others to sink their claws and fangs into what remained.

"It's a shame he was already dead," Yung murmured.

"Maybe next time," Saleh replied.

General Rashid finished his call and joined the group. He seemed distracted and barely took notice of the spectacle taking place down in the quarry.

"Have the medics reached Shah yet?" Saleh asked him.

Rashid nodded. "He'd passed out by the time they got to him, but he's conscious now. They should have him here by nightfall."

"Is there something else?" Faryad asked.

"We may have silenced Karimi," Rashid told the others, "but somehow they've managed to come up with a lead from the autopsies."

Saleh's countenance darkened. He'd chosen to feed O'Brien to the leopards as payback for what the Americans had done with the bodies of his fallen comrades—to have his vengeance tempered was unsettling.

"What did they find out?" he asked.

"They know where your men have been safe-havened across the border," Rashid told him.

"Balqhat?"

Rashid nodded; Saleh cursed.

"I don't have any details yet," Rashid said, "but they're certain to take some kind of action. And they're apt to do it quickly, before word gets back and the rest of your men have a chance to leave."

The men fell silent, coming to grips with this latest development. Faryad let his attention stray back to the quarry, where several vultures had flown down and taken roost on the limbs of a dead tree overlooking the leopards' feeding frenzy. He turned the situation in Balqhat over in his mind, and it wasn't long before a plan began to take shape.

"There's no reason we can't act just as quickly," he finally told the others. "If we do, we might be able to turn this into an opportunity."

BROGNOLA'S CIGAR WAS BACK out as he made his way into the Computer Room. He rolled it between his left fingers and took a quick sip of coffee brewed by Aaron Kurtzman. He grimaced slightly at its bitter taste.

"Okay, what do we have, people?" he called out to the cybercrew. Kurtzman and his three colleagues were busy at work. Price would be rejoining them shortly, once she finished touring the grounds to check for further storm damage.

"Bits and pieces," Tokaido told Brognola. "Balqhat's looking like our top priority. Striker's chomping at the bit to get there ASAP while the trail's still hot."

"I'd say that's the right call," the SOG chief concurred. "The big issue is getting him there. The way security's been compromised at Bagram, Striker's probably wary of going through channels there."

"You got that right," Kurtzman replied.

"I just checked in with McCarter over in Srinagar," Delahunt reported. "Phoenix is working the ground for the next couple days, so he said they can spare Jack."

Jack Grimaldi was Stony Man's chief pilot, a combat-hardened flyboy brought into the organization years ago on Bolan's recommendation. He'd shuttled Phoenix Force to India earlier in the week and had remained to help them close in on a faction of the Jammu Kashmir Liberation Front plotting an attack on U.S. delegates monitoring cease-fire talks at the disputed region's capital. Brognola didn't need to check a map to realize that Srinagar was just a short jet flight away from Bagram Air Force Base.

"Good option," he said. "Get him in the air, pronto."

"Sure thing," Delahunt said.

"We'll need a place where Striker can rendezvous with him off base," Brognola went on. "A decent chopper would come in handy, too, if there's going be an insertion."

"Already greasing the skids on that," Tokaido said. "CIA wants in, and they're at least once removed from Bagram."

"All right, then," Brognola said. "Now, what about these other bits and pieces?"

"We've got eleven dead at the base," Kurtzman reported. "Two from the control tower, six from the fuel depot and three at the medical center, counting Karimi."

"And then there's the two men who helped Shah make his getaway," Wethers added. "Profiler flagged only one of them, and there wasn't enough to peg him as a high-level threat."

"It wouldn't have mattered," Brognola reminded the other man. "By the time we sent out word, they were already in motion."

"That's true," Wethers said. "But still, I'm disappointed the databases didn't raise a few more red flags."

"Profiler's still a work in progress," Kurtzman reminded his colleague. "We just need to keep beefing it up."

"While you're doing that," Brognola said, "maybe you can go a little deeper on this Shah fellow."

"Been there, done that," Kurtzman replied. "According to AI, Shah had a good work record and was Mr. Popularity around the base. He was getting trusty privileges in terms of being able to move around on his own."

"The wrong call, obviously," Brognola said. He stuck his cigar in a corner of his mouth and set down his coffee cup. "I don't care how charming he was, somebody had to have dropped the ball for him to be able to smuggle a gun in."

"We're running a trace on it," Tokaido said, "but the serial numbers were filed off, so you gotta figure it was black market."

"What about his references?" Brognola asked. "Workers there need to be vouched for before anyone even bothers with background checks, right?"

Kurtzman nodded, pecking at his keyboard to call up the growing file on Shah. "His previous job was running deliveries for an outfit in Kabul that services the cafeterias at Bagram along with most of the ANA bases. His job application had half the company brass down as references along with a procurement officer at the base and a few Afghan military honchos."

"Is AI questioning the procurement officer?"

"As we speak," Kurtzman said. "I'm trying to patch through to Personnel at the supplier, too. Ditto with ANA."

"These honchos you mentioned," Brognola said. "Do we have names?"

Kurtzman smiled at the big Fed. "I was saving that for the punch line," he said. "Yeah, we have names, and I'm liking one of them as the guy we ought to be focusing on."

"Somebody involved with the Taliban routs they've been pulling off," Brognola guessed.

"The boss wins a Kewpie doll!" Kurtzman said. "Turns out Shah's main squeeze with ANA is the same guy who ran that raid the other night near Jalalabad."

"General Rashid?"

"That's the one," Kurtzman said.

Brognola stopped his pacing. "This could be the break we've been looking for."

"Big time," Kurtzman said. "And if Rashid's in bed with the Taliban, it opens up some damn interesting theories about why ANA's been having such a field day taking them down."

"Not only that," Tokaido interjected. "Rashid's enough in the loop at Bagram to know about troop movements. If he's been ratting to the Taliban, it'd explain why we've been taking it on the chin over there so much lately."

Brognola nodded and turned back to Kurtzman. "I take it you're already following through on this."

"Running some checks," Kurtzman confirmed. "Of course, it'd help if we could haul him in for a friendly little interrogation."

"We don't know where he is?"

"'In the field,'" Kurtzman said. "That's all I can get. The guy keeps a lid on his whereabouts like he's Bin Laden or something. Apparently he claims it's to give him better leverage against the enemy."

"I'll buy that," Brognola said. "The question at this point is, who does he consider the enemy? The Taliban or us...?"

LIKE ALL THE OTHERS detained at the bazaar outside Bagram Air Base, Nawid Pradhan had undergone prolonged questioning at the hands of the Americans. He'd fallen under even more scrutiny because his job application listed Shah as a reference. It was likely he'd still be in custody if not for the soldier in the Humvee who'd tried to get him onto the base. The officer had convinced Pradhan's interrogators that if he had been part of Shah's plot, the missing Afghan would have acknowledged knowing him so that he could get inside the base. Pradhan still had no idea what Shah had done, but he knew it had to have had something to do with the explosions, and he suspected, for whatever reason, that Shah had turned on his benefactors. He knew, also, that at least some of the demonstrators had been in collusion with Shah. What other explanation could there be for the way they'd aided in his escape?

After what had seemed an eternity, a carload of government officials from Kabul had finally arrived along with lawyers protesting the detention. Faced with the prospects of fueling even greater political furor over Western presence in the country, the troop interrogators had relented. Pradhan had been given back his application and allowed to leave the bazaar with the others. He'd gotten a ride back to Kabul with one of the merchants.

Now, as evening settled over the Afghan capital, Pradhan found himself standing before a rubble-strewed, weed-choked plot of land near the market square. It was the first time in more than sixteen years that the Kabul native had returned to the site. Back then, he'd lived in one of the better units of the apartment complex that stood on the property, just a short walk from his job as a computer specialist for the Department of Internal Services. He'd been well-paid for the long hours he worked helping configure firewalls and other protective programs to aid the government's forays into Internet-based communications. There had been talk of a promotion and a raise in salary before that fateful day. The Taliban had made one of their ongoing attacks on Kabul, targeting the apartment complex, which housed, along with Pradhan's family and many of his closest friends, several American families whose parents worked at the U.S. consulate. Pradhan's hip had been crushed by falling debris when the building collapsed, but the greater loss had been that of his two children, who were among the fifty-four fatalities.

Their lives turned asunder, Pradhan and his wife fled the country after burying their children, taking flight across the border to the refugee camps of Pakistan. It had been a torturous exile, a time of inhumane living conditions with few opportunities to earn a living. Pradhan had stooped to begging, feeling his soul shrink with every plea. After years of degradation, he'd become a sorry shell of his former self, resigned to the fate the Taliban had forced on him. Others, driven to the brink by despair and anger, had turned on one another. There were riots in the camps, and one terrible night Pradhan had come back from his begging to find his wife raped and beaten. The next day they'd packed their few belongings and crossed back into their homeland, hopeful there might be truth to the rumors of government assistance to those who'd been forced into exile.

Upon his return to Kabul, however, all that Pradhan had been offered was a bureaucratic runaround. His contacts within the government had all moved on, and there was no one to attest to his work experience. He filled out form after form, only to see them lost in a sea of red tape. Finally he'd given up and taken matters into his own hands, going door-to-door until he found work, such as it was, at the Internet café, supplemented by his weekly forays to the bazaar, where, by chance, he'd run into Shah.

Staring at the empty lot, Pradhan recalled how he'd pulled Bodhi Shah from the burning ruins of the apartment complex and helped him track down his children, including young Mehrab, then only a teenager. He'd risked his own life to come to Bodhi's aid, expecting nothing in return, and it had shamed him to use the rescue for leverage once he'd learned that Shah worked at the Army base. But Pradhan knew he had all but run out of chances to better his life, so he'd swallowed his pride and begged Shah to help him. What a mistake that had been!

It was getting late. The storm threatening Kabul earlier in the day had skirted the Afghanistan capital but left behind a cold front, and Pradhan's new clothes, now tainted with dirt and grime, did a poorer job than his old rags at fending off the chill in the air. Pradhan shivered as he finally turned his back on the deserted lot and headed for the market square. He despised his wardrobe and all the foolishness it reminded him of. How could he have been so gullible as to think his circumstances were about to change for the better? If anything, his life was now even more in shambles.

The market square had closed for the night, but Pradhan foraged through a few trash bins for something to bring back to his wife. Afterward, he left the city behind and limped past one of the many dilapidated shantytowns scattered about the surrounding foothills. He was still shivering, but he took what consolation he could in the way the bracing cold numbed the pain in his arthritic hip. It took his mind off his hunger, as well, curbing any temptation to raid the provisions he'd taken from one of the waste bins and then stashed in a ragged burlap sack. A heel of stale bread, an onion and three well-bruised pears. Some feast! he thought to himself bitterly.

A few hundred yards past the makeshift tenements, Pradhan started up a narrow dirt road that wound through a gauntlet of hawthorn and wild rosebushes deeper into the foothills, where his wife, along with a few dozen other displaced Tajiks, sought refuge from the harsh elements in a series of caves and abandoned mine shafts. The path before him was dimly illuminated by a near-full moon, and Pradhan was puzzled when he noticed a set of tire tracks burrowed deep into the loose soil. He'd made this same trek every day during the three months since moving into the caves, and this was the first time he'd seen any trace of a vehicle larger than a bicycle making use of the road. Pradhan wasn't sure what to make of it, but he found himself lengthening his stride with a sense of foreboding.

The Afghan had hobbled up to where the road leveled off when he first saw the truck, parked in a clearing next to the foundation of what had once been a storehouse for mined ore. The vehicle was the size of a small moving van, painted a military shade of olive green with a taut canvas shell enclosing the rear bed. There was no one behind the wheel, but the engine was running and a cloud of exhaust trailed upward from the tailpipe, half-shrouding a man who stood next to the lowered tailgate. The man clutched a rifle. Pradhan's first thought was that the Americans had somehow learned this was his "home" and had come to question him more about his relationship with Shah. But as he drew closer, he saw that the man was Afghan, dressed in shepherd's clothing. His features were Pashtun, and though he wore a woolen cap instead of a telltale black turban, Pradhan feared the man belonged to those responsible for his dire straits.

Taliban.

Heart racing, Pradhan veered off the path and sought cover in the nearby brush. His hip throbbed and perspiration beaded his forehead, not only from the exertion of his uphill climb, but also from a growing fear. Carefully, he unslung his burlap sack and weighed his options. What was he to do? Run for help? There was no one to go to. And run? He could barely walk! Fight? With what?

Pradhan glanced around him and snatched up a small rock. He clutched it tightly in his fist, at the same time scoffing inwardly at his foolishness. A rock against a rifle? What good would that be? He might as well go up against the gunman with his bagful of discarded food.

Moments later, Pradhan spotted movement near the base of the mountain. A handful of men were heading away from the nearest caves, each of them dressed similarly to the man guarding the truck. Their rifles were slung over their shoulders, freeing their hands to haul bodies, all of them women and children. As they drew near the truck, Pradhan spotted two more men up in the bed, crouched near the tailgate. One by one, the human cargo was passed up to them and they dragged the bodies inside, carefully setting them down alongside one another.

When he recognized his wife being unceremoniously shuttled up into the truck, Pradhan let out a cry and lurched to his feet. Acting on impulse, he threw the rock with all his might, then stood, quaking with rage, as he watched it glance harmlessly off the truck's rear quarter panel.

"Why?" he roared in his native Dari, shaking his now-empty fist as he staggered toward the truck. "We've done nothing to you! Why are you doing this?"

The man with the rifle glanced at Pradhan and slowly leveled the weapon, taking aim at the refugee. Before he could pull the trigger, however, one of his comrades reached out and pushed the barrel to one side.

"Fire that thing and you'll just draw attention!" the second man grated. "I'll take care of him!"

When Pradhan saw the second man draw a pistol from his web holster, he stopped in the road and glared defiantly.

"Go ahead!" he shouted.

"Stop shouting," the gunman warned as he drew closer.

"You've killed my wife!" he railed on. "What do I have to live for?"

The gunman raised his pistol. Pradhan heard a faint *pffffft* above the sound of the truck's engine. He groaned as he felt something bore through the thin fabric of his shirt and plow into his flesh, just below the shoulder blade. The impact knocked him backward with just enough force that he lost his balance and sprawled into the dirt. He'd never been shot before, but he'd always assumed a bullet at such close range would inflict far more pain. What he'd felt instead was little more than a faint jab. His mind raced. Was he in shock? Was adrenaline overriding the pain?

Whatever the case, Pradhan felt that he owed it to his wife to at least die fighting. As he tried to stand back up, however, he lost his equilibrium and swooned back to his knees. He felt as if the earth beneath him had turned into quicksand and was pulling him down. He became light-headed and when he tried to shout at his attacker, his tongue flapped errantly and the words came out garbled and incoherent. Pins of light pulsated and began to swirl randomly across his field of vision. By the time the lights gave way to an all-consuming darkness, Pradhan had collapsed to the ground, his face pressed against the cold dirt.

"We haven't killed anybody," the gunman assured Pradhan as he stood over him, holstering his tranquilizer gun. The man wasn't with the Taliban. It was ANA General Zahir Rashid. "Not yet, at least."

12

"I'd hate to see the other guy," Jack Grimaldi said, eyeing the swollen facial bruises Bolan had sustained during his hand-to-hand skirmish with Shah a few hours earlier.

"For the time being, you won't have to worry about that," the Executioner said as the two men shook hands. "He's still MIA."

Grimaldi had just disembarked the Eclipse 500 jet that had whisked him from Srinagar to Kabul in a little less than three hours after he'd received his flight orders from Stony Man. The ace pilot had touched down at the capital's international airport and taxied to a remote hangar purportedly leased by a commercial delivery outfit called Eurasia Air Cargo. The facility was, in fact, one of the CIA's primary nerve centers in Afghanistan.

"You managed to shake your Bagram buddies?" Grimaldi asked as they circled the hangar.

Bolan nodded. "They think I'm doing a follow-up on some of the demonstrators from the trucks we intercepted. I told them I'd be back later to go over plans for an insertion into Balqhat."

"They're in for a long wait," Grimaldi stated.

"It's better this way," Bolan said.

"Anything come out of the interrogations?"

"Not really," Bolan confided. "Half of them clammed up and the rest either played dumb or threw out red herrings hoping to send us on a wild-goose chase."

"I love those," Grimaldi deadpanned.

There were a handful of cargo planes parked behind the hangar along with a small fleet of delivery trucks. CIA agents doubling as route carriers were loading parcels from a loading dock into several of the vehicles. Standing near them was a clean-shaved, crew-cut man in his late forties. When he spotted Bolan and Grimaldi, he waved them over, then barked a few words into his cell phone. By the time the Stony Man operatives reached the man, the large door to one of the hangar's service bays had begun to retract, revealing a two-seat Kiowa Warrior. The assault chopper's weapon pylons were rigged with seven Hyrdra-70 rockets and a .50-caliber fixed forward machine gun.

"Evening, gents." Agent Zane Anderson's Texan drawl was as thick as his taut neck. "I'm told you're in a hurry, so we'll spare the code words and secret handshakes."

"Works for me," Bolan said.

"I was kinda hoping for the third degree myself," Grimaldi said.

"Sorry to disappoint," Anderson told him. "I got your security clearance and a no-questions-asked order straight from the Oval Office. I don't care who you are so long as you kick some Taliban ass and bring the bird back in one piece."

It was the second time Bolan had heard the phrase "kick some Taliban ass." He stared at Anderson. "Did you know a Captain O'Brien by any chance?"

Anderson nodded. "Yeah, I knew Howitzer. Poor bastard. I understand part of your mission is to track down his body."

"We'll do our best," the Executioner promised.

Bolan had yet to hear from the Farm regarding his suspicions that the Predator downed over Bagram might've once been part of the CIA's arsenal, but before he could ask Anderson about missing drones, his cell phone vibrated. He detoured from the dock to take the call.

It was Brognola.

"Are you and JG airborne yet?" the SOG chief asked.

"We will be soon enough," Bolan said.

"You might want to step on it," Brognola told him. "We just glommed onto a communiqué between AI and Special Ops at Bagram. They've just sent a team to Balqhat without you."

Airspace over Parvan Province, Afghanistan

CAPTAIN ROB KITT sat quietly in the cargo bay of the UH-60 Black Hawk that had just taken to the air with the same six Special Ops commandos that had accompanied him on Operation Rat Trap the previous night. The others were equally solemn, some busying themselves with their weapons, others staring pensively out the bay windows at the cloud-strewed night sky.

It hadn't been Kitt's intention to set out without the man he knew only as Special Agent Cooper. If anything, he would have preferred it if the mysterious warrior had returned to the base in time to join his crew—but *time* was of the essence. Fresh sat-cam footage from surveillance satellites deployed over the Pakistan tribal region indicated suspicious activity at a farm on the outskirts of Balqhat. A sequence of photos had shown three large trucks negotiating a narrow mountain road leading to the village, and in an enlarged shot taken shortly after the trucks had reached their destination, nearly fifty men could be seen congregating around the vehicles, most of them carrying what looked to be Kalashnikov AK-47s. The implication was clear—the Taliban had somehow been informed about the discovery of their clandestine base and were intent on evacuation.

"What's the chance we'll get to them before they relocate?" one of Kitt's men called out, breaking the silence.

"Depends on the cloud cover," Kitt responded. "We were lucky to get the sat-cam shots that we did. If it gets any more overcast, there'll be no way to track their movements."

"Those cam shots were taken a while ago," another of the soldiers ventured, "and we're still an hour away from the border. With that kind of head start, they could be just about anywhere, and we don't even know which way they were going."

"We've got a break on that front," Kitt said, tapping the detailed topographical map spread across his lap. "Balqhat is way the hell out in the boonies. The only way out is the same way those trucks got in, and the road's nothing more than a glorified mule track. Figure in all the switchbacks, and you gotta figure they're moving at a snail's pace. Odds are we'll get to them before they make it out of the mountains."

"Sounds good to me," yet another commando said. "After what those bastards have pulled, I'm ready to dish out some industrial-strength payback."

"Same here," the second soldier said. "I just wish this bird came with a little firepower. Six of us going up against fifty of them… I don't think my bookie's laying many bets on this one."

"You're probably right," Kitt told him. "Hell, those poor suckers don't stand a chance."

The other soldiers broke out laughing. Kitt played along, cracking a wide smirk. *Nothing like a little gallows humor to ease the tension,* he thought.

The laughter was short-lived. When it ended, an uneasy silence fell over the group again. Kitt deliberated whether or not this might be a good time to let his men know there was a chance they'd have backup in the form of a pair of Apache gunships. He finally decided against it. The other choppers had already been designated for an assignment farther to the north, where informants claimed yet another Taliban force was planning to blow up the Salang Tunnel. At the time of their takeoff, Kitt was still uncertain if the Apaches would be diverted.

The captain turned slightly and stared ahead out through the cargo windows. Off in the distance, he could see the rising peaks of the Safed Koh Range. They would be there soon, and once they cleared the range, they would be across the border, where, as he'd warned Special Agent Cooper, one ran the risk of running afoul of not only the Taliban, but also tribal warlords and overzealous forces within the Pakistan military.

This is it, he told himself, steeling his courage. Even as he was doing so, his right hand drifted to his chest, tapping the breast pocket of his camo jacket. There, sealed inside a silver cigarette case inherited from his father, were pictures of his wife and three children, as well as a handwritten letter telling them how his devotion to his country was surpassed only by his love for his family. It was his intention—and great hope—that the letter would wind up in the trash on the day he received his honorable discharge and boarded a plane back to the States. But there were times when he felt that the letter might well end up being his last communication with those he'd left behind in service to his country.

This was one of those times.

BROGNOLA HUNG UP the security phone and turned to the others in the Annex Computer Room.

"It's done," he told them.

The SOG director had just spoken with the President, asking him to step in as commander in chief and temporarily rescind a standing policy at Bagram Air Base to apprise the Afghanistan National Army of allied troop movements within the country.

"How'd it go over?" Price asked.

"He has the same reservations we do," Brognola conceded. "That shared info's supposed to cut down on the chances of men getting cut down by friendly fire."

"Yeah," Delahunt countered, "but if Rashid's passing that info along to the Taliban, it's not friendly fire our guys have to worry about."

"That's still a big 'if,'" Brognola said, "but until we track him down or can at least corroborate that he's a turncoat, I think it's best we err on the side of caution."

"Agreed," Price said. "And I know it's small consolation, but if we're right about this, it could mean AI's clean along with everyone else in the loop at Bagram."

"That would be a load off everyone's mind," Brognola agreed. "Time will tell. If we start carrying out missions over there without being sabotaged at every turn, it'll be a pretty clear sign that all those setbacks the past few weeks have been orchestrated through ANA."

"I'm a little concerned about that," Wethers interjected.

"How so?" Brognola asked.

"This cross-sharing of deployment intel was for ANA's benefit as well as ours," Wethers said. "A blackout's going to increase the risk we'll mistake one of their field squads for Taliban."

"I'm sure it'll get a little dicey," Brognola conceded, "but it has to be done. And there could be an upside to this, too. Once we make it clear we've detected a security breach, hopefully they'll step in and clean house on their own. It's not like their whole bushel is rotten, and they'll have to figure it's in their best interests to weed out the bad apples ASAP."

"On the other hand," Kurtzman countered, "maybe they'll just take offense and stonewall."

"I don't see that happening," Brognola said.

"No? Think about it," Kurtzman stated. "If ANA's ultimate goal is to get us out of the country, it'd be easy enough to put the Ugly American spin on this and step up calls for withdrawal on the grounds that we're taking too much unilateral action."

"That would be a mistake."

Kurtzman shrugged. "What can I say? You throw politics into the mix, anything can happen."

Price glanced over at Tokaido, who was following the conversation with a look of concern.

"Something on your mind?" she asked him.

"Just thinking," he said. "This blackout's too late as far as what's going down over there as we speak. If we're right about

Rashid passing intel to the Taliban, they might already know Bagram's sending men to Balqhat. That throws any element of surprise out the window."

"Let's hope that's not the case," Price said, "because it'd mean Striker could be heading into an ambush, too."

Safed Koh Mountain Range, Afghanistan

"This won't be the first time I've done this," the Taliban combat medic assured Shah, as he clamped his cold fingers to either side of the wounded man's jaw. "And the longer we wait, the greater the chances for more complications. Now hold still and try to relax."

The two men were seated on the rear flatbed of an all-terrain vehicle, an electric cart similar to the one Shah used to make deliveries back at Bagram Air Base. The ATV was equipped with larger balloon tires, however, as well as hydraulic shocks to minimize jarring as it navigated rugged terrain like that of the chiseled-out tunnels through which Shah had been transported after escaping his pursuers back near Kabul. One of Aden Saleh's most-trusted lieutenants, Arsalan Kali, was at the wheel and had stopped the vehicle moments ago when Shah had begun to have trouble breathing.

Once he was certain that Shah had let his jaw go as lax as possible, the medic shifted his grip. There was a faint pop as Shah's jaw slipped back into place. The manipulation triggered a jolt of pain so severe that the Taliban sympathizer blacked out. When he came to a few seconds later, the cart was moving and the medic had pressed an ice pack to the side of his face. Shah realized that he could now move his jaw enough to speak.

"It worked," he whispered hoarsely.

"Do you remember passing out any time before this?" the medic asked.

"When I was thrown from the truck," Shah said. "And once, maybe twice, while I was in the boat."

"He might have a concussion," the medic called up to Kali. "We should probably divert to Daruntah. I can sneak him into the clinic there."

"No!" Shah protested.

"We already passed the turnoff," Kali said without taking his eyes off the darkened tunnel ahead of him. "We'll be at the safe house in less than an hour. Let's see how he's doing then."

"I'll be fine," Shah insisted.

When he tried to sit up, the medic gently pushed him down.

"Relax. You've done your part."

"I want to do more," Shah said.

"What you can do is be quiet and stay still," Kali commanded. "That's an order."

Shah scowled as he lay back in the ATV. His headache was gone, and though he was still sore he doubted he'd broken any bones in the fall from the truck. The last thing he wanted was to find himself sidetracked at some clinic. Not only had he just proved himself, but he'd also blown his cover at the air base and was free to more actively take part in the Taliban cause. He wanted to take full advantage of the opportunity as soon as he could.

A quarter of a mile farther down the tunnel, the ATV rounded the bend and came upon a lamp-lit checkpoint. The area was more than twice the width of the tunnel and several feet higher. Three soldiers sat on rocks near several crates stocked with weapons and provisions. Nearby, another officer stood next to a laddered shaft extending to the surface. The officer was on a cable phone linked to Saleh's headquarters at the opium farm.

"We'll tend to it," the officer said. He hung up the phone and eyed the men in the ATV.

"You're just in time," he told Kali. "We have an assignment."

"So do I," Kali replied.

"This is more important," the officer responded. "The Americans are sending an aerial force to Balqhat. They'll be passing over us any minute."

"I thought we wanted them to show up there," Kali said.

"Not until we've had a chance to fully prepare for them," the officer said. One of the soldiers had already raided one of the crates for an RPG-7 rocket launcher. The officer reached out and took the weapon, adding, "Besides, there are at least two helicopters headed there. We only need one of them to make it to Balqhat."

13

"Your call," Grimaldi told Bolan as he powered the OH-58 Kiowa Warrior over the mountainous terrain of the Safed Koh Range. The Stony Man pilot had just fielded a patched-in call from the Farm advising them that the Taliban might have been forewarned of their mission to Balqhat. Kurtzman had thrown out the option of having the men turn back.

"You have to ask?" the Executioner replied.

Grimaldi smirked, then tapped his headphone.

"It's unanimous here, Bear," he informed Kurtzman. "Cue up some Springsteen, 'cause like the Boss says, it's no retreat and no surrender."

"We're not surprised," Kurtzman replied. "Good luck to you both."

"We'll take it," Grimaldi replied. "Over and out."

Staring down at the mountains, Bolan sought landmarks, finally spotting the peak beneath which he and Captain O'Brien had been on stakeout when the Taliban had made their first move the night before.

"Full circle," he murmured.

"What's that?"

Bolan shook his head, then pointed upward through the slanted windshield. "Cloud bank ahead. We might as well make use of it."

Grimaldi jockeyed the controls and took the chopper up another few hundred feet. Before they could reach the clouds, however, both men saw two faint streaks of light shoot upward from one of the mountain peaks more than a mile ahead of them. Seconds later, an explosion turned the clouds bright. A ball of fire appeared and quickly began to separate, raining down like a meteor shower.

Grimaldi cursed. "They just got one of us."

Bolan nodded grimly—Captain Kitt's squad had been taken out in one fateful blow. It brought him little consolation when he realized that, if not for his diversionary trip into Kabul, he might have well been aboard the chopper that now fell in fiery pieces across the mountain slopes below.

"Course of action?" Grimaldi queried.

Bolan's blue eyes turned cold as he stared in the direction from which the rockets had been fired. He was too far away to see any sign of the attackers, but the Executioner hoped they were still out in the open. Readying himself before the console linked to the Kiowa's outer weapon pods, he said, "Balqhat will have to wait."

"I'M NOT SURE whose shot it was," the Taliban soldier said, as he stood alongside Arsalan Kali on the ridgeline near the mouth of the tunnel through which they'd reached the surface. A pungent, vaporous ribbon of smoke trailed from both of their RPG launchers.

"It doesn't matter," Kali replied sternly, eyes on the burning remains of the downed chopper. There would be no need to hike down to the wreckage to finish off any survivors—he was certain everyone on board had been killed. "It's done."

The men started back toward the tunnel, then stopped in their tracks, alerted by the sound of another chopper. Glancing up, they saw the Kiowa Warrior float into view, headed their way. Kali quickly dropped to a crouch, feeding another rocket into his launcher.

"What are you doing?" the other soldier said. "We were supposed to just take out one of them and let the other cross the border."

"Why let someone else have the glory?" Kali said.

"But there is a plan."

"Plans change."

Kali poised the launcher on his shoulder and put his eye to the scope. But before he could draw bead on his target, the Kiowa's machine gun fired, raking the mountainside with .50-caliber bullets. Kali caught two of the slugs and keeled to the ground, howling. The other soldier had been spared, for the moment. Casting aside his launcher, he scrambled to the tunnel and began to lower himself down the shaft.

Kali, however, wasn't about to run. He ignored his wounds and slowly struggled back to his knees, despite the blood drenching his clothes. As an involuntary cough brought up blood from his chest, he knew he was dying, which only hardened his resolve to annihilate those who'd fired at him. Hands trembling, he tried to steady the RPG on his shoulder. It was no use. His vision had already begun to cloud, and he felt as if he'd been suddenly immersed in cold water. Shivering, blood trailing down his chin, he watched a small bead of flame emanate from one of the approaching chopper's weapon pods. It was an image he would take with him to his grave, as moments later his heart gave out and he collapsed to the ground, even as the Kiowa's M229 HE warhead whooshed past, detonating on impact with the mountainside directly behind him. The 17-pound charge packed enough force to create a tremor that dislodged loose rocks and boulders as far as halfway up the mountain. Bits of rubble merged together, creating a small landslide. In all, several tons of rock descended upon the man. Within seconds, he'd been partially entombed by debris. Buried alongside him was the mouth of the tunnel. Kali would never know it, but his foolhardiness had inadvertently given his comrades below a chance to be spared his fate.

GRIMALDI MADE several passes over the avalanche while Bolan kept an eye open for more Taliban. He could see someone's half-buried body beneath the fallen rubble, but spotted no other enemy presence.

"If anyone's left, they've gone underground," the Executioner said.

"Gives them home-court advantage if we go after them."

Bolan nodded. "I'm sure they'd like that."

"Leave them be, then?"

"For the moment, at least," Bolan said. "Let's check on the chopper."

Grimaldi banked the Kiowa and tipped its nose downward, allowing Bolan to direct the searchlight at a stretch of mountainside where the remnants of the other helicopter had gone down. Most of the fires had gone out. Bolan spotted two bodies amid the scattered debris, both partially dismembered from the force of the rocket blasts. It was a grisly sight. Bolan had witnessed carnage countless times on the battlefield and though he'd hardened himself to such sights, there was a part of him that couldn't help but feel a sense of loss, especially when he knew the victims.

Or did he?

"Come in a little," Bolan told Grimaldi. "I want a better look at the fuselage."

Grimaldi brought the Kiowa closer to the mountainside. Rotor wash began to stir up loose sand, but not enough to obstruct Bolan's view. He directed the searchlight to the largest intact piece of the downed chopper. The section was twisted and charred by fire but not beyond the point where the Executioner could discern its markings and design.

"An Apache," he said.

"Are you sure?" Grimaldi asked. "We were told a whole squad was flying to Balqhat. No way could they all cram into that thing."

"You're right," Bolan said. "Aaron said Bagram might send backup, though."

"Then there's a chance your guys are still alive."

Bolan nodded.

"And if that's the case," he said, "they've still got backup."

Spin Range, Nangarhar Province, Afghanistan

"THEY'RE ON TO ME," General Rashid said, clicking off his cell phone.

"What makes you say that?" Faryad asked.

"ANA's been told they'll no longer be notified of allied troops' movements," Rashid said, his face flushed with anger. "There's only one explanation."

The two men were standing next to a concealed helipad tucked into a large cavity in the base of the mountains, just uphill from the quarry where Captain O'Brien's corpse had been fed to the snow leopards. Out on the pad, some of the men who had earlier been working the opium fields were carefully removing a large hemp-woven net draped over a vintage UH-1 Iroquois transport chopper. The Huey, which bore a freshly applied set of forged U.S. military decals, had been bought two years ago at auction by a KGB shadow company and rendered operable thanks to Yung and the same team responsible for salvaging the Predator. Resting on the pad next to the Huey was a smaller, similarly acquired Bell 206 LongRanger. Since their inception, the Taliban had always preferred to fight their battles on the ground, but there were times when it was obviously more advantageous to take to the air. This was one of those times.

Just downhill from the helipad, the homeless refugees Rashid's men had abducted from the caves near Kabul stood next to the truck that had brought them to Saleh's compound. Except for Pradhan, the captives were all women and children and they stood shivering in the cold, some still groggy from the effects of the tranquilizer darts. Two soldiers stood guard over them with AK-47s, and once the netting had been removed from the Huey, the captives were directed to march to the helipad. Pradhan, however, was kept behind.

Rashid and Faryad were discussing the implications of the U.S.-NATO blackout when Saleh jogged up the path from his quarters.

"My men just brought down one of the helicopters headed for Balqhat," he told them.

"Praise Allah," Rashid said with a trace of cynicism.

"But a second chopper took out one of my men before flying off."

"Bound for Balqhat, we hope," Faryad said.

"That would be my guess," Saleh replied.

"We'll be doing a lot of guessing from here on in regarding the enemy," Rashid said. He went on to tell Saleh about the blackout notification when one of his men called out from the helipad, asking for confirmation to start boarding the prisoners onto the Huey.

"Yes!" Rashid snapped. "All of them except for him," he added, pointing to Pradhan. "Bring him over."

While the general's head was turned, Saleh and Faryad exchanged a quick, telling glance. No words needed to be exchanged. It was clear they were both thinking the same thing: Rashid had suddenly become a liability.

When Rashid turned back, Faryad assured the general, "This will only be a temporary setback. We'll find another way to learn what we need to know about their movements. For now, though, we need to see things through in Balqhat."

"Agreed," Rashid said.

Indicating the prisoners, he continued, "They'll get there in plenty of time, especially if the Americans take the bait and detour once they've crossed the border."

"They'll fall for it," Faryad predicted. "And when they do, they'll learn that we know how to build a better rat trap."

"I think we already showed them that last night," Saleh said. He glanced over Rashid's shoulder and gestured at the male prisoner being brought to them. "Why's he staying behind?"

"We need only women and children," Rashid reminded the Taliban leader. "Besides, he might be of use to you."

"How so?"

"Is Yung still having trouble cracking the access code to that field computer?" Rashid asked.

"Yes, but in time he'll get through."

Rashid reached into his pocket and pulled out the job application found on Pradhan after the computer specialist had been taken captive. Handing the application to Saleh, the general said, "Maybe he'll get through sooner instead of later if he has some assistance."

14

"Over there!" Bolan called out shortly after Grimaldi brought the Kiowa Warrior below the cloud line. The Stony Man warriors had just crossed the border and were approaching the base of the long mountain road linking Balqhat with Indus Highway, the main thoroughfare running through Pakistan's Federally Administered Tribal Areas. Up ahead, the UH-60 Black Hawk carrying Captain Rob Kitt's Special Ops force hovered in place high above the intersection. As Bolan took in the surrounding airspace as well as the landscape below, it quickly became clear why Kitt's men had yet to make a move. Grimaldi saw it, too, and sized up the situation.

"We've been set up," he said.

Facing off with Kitt's Black Hawk was a trio of heavily armed AH-1 Cobra gunships, mainstays of the Pakistan air force. Like the Black Hawk, the Cobras were also in a holding pattern, their Chain Guns and stub-winged missiles aimed at Kitt's helicopter. Soon one of the choppers had placed the Kiowa in its sites, as well.

The only thing more unexpected than the aerial standoff was the strange, almost surreal tableau on the ground below. The three trucks that had shown up on earlier sat-cam images of Balqhat were idling just shy of the intersection, smoke trailing from their exhaust pipes as well as from scattered flares bathing the roadway with a flickering glow. The tailgates of all three trucks were down, but from the air there was no way to tell if there were more Taliban forces concealed in the freight holds. Encircling the vehicles were nearly two dozen women and children. Some of the latter were mere infants clutched in their mothers' arms. Their vigil was clearly involuntary and the Executioner could see the barrels of Kalashnikov assault rifles poking out the cab windows of each truck.

"Human shields," Bolan murmured.

"The Taliban's good at that," Grimaldi said.

Compounding matters, more flares set off in the surrounding hills cast an eerie light on three large groups of men armed with handguns and assault rifles. The weapons were all aimed skyward at both the Kiowa and Black Hawk.

"Nothing like rolling out the red carpet," Grimaldi murmured.

Bolan was still assessing the situation when a radio call crackled through his headset. It was Kitt.

"That you, Cooper?"

"Affirmative," Bolan said.

"We were expecting a couple Apaches."

"At least one of them didn't make it," Bolan reported. "I don't know about the other."

There was a moment of silence, then Kitt said, "We've got a situation on our hands."

"One they were hoping for from the looks of it."

"I heard from one of the birds," Kitt reported. "They say this is an internal matter. We're supposed to butt out."

"And let them handle it, I suppose," Bolan said.

"That's their take," Kitt said. "If that means the way they've handled things up to now, I'm guessing a slap on the wrist, and then everybody goes back to business as usual."

"Maybe so."

On closer inspection, Bolan saw that the tires of the first two vehicles had been flattened. Behind them, the third truck had stopped just shy of a crudely fashioned spike strip made of barbed-wire wrapped around a board studded with jagged bits of scrap metal. "Those men on the hillside," he asked Kitt, "are they the ones who stopped the trucks?"

"That's my understanding," Kitt replied. "They're a rival tribe to the one in Balqhat."

"They're working with the Cobras, then?"

"I think it's more of a common-enemy thing," Kitt said. "Apparently some of the Taliban bolted from the trucks before we got here. The flares hadn't been lit, so we don't have any numbers. No telling at this point if they're still close by or if they made a run for it."

Bolan surveyed the roadside flanking the trucks. Beyond a narrow shoulder, the land pitched sharply upward and was thick with tall brush, all of it cloaked in darkness. If more Taliban were still lurking in the vegetation, it only added to the volatility of the standoff.

"Any suggestions?" Kitt asked.

Bolan eyed the women and children. He knew a conflagration would put them in even more jeopardy. It wasn't a risk he was willing to take.

"Let's start back," he said, "but only as far as the cloud bank. I don't want to just wash our hands of this."

"I'm with you," said Kitt. "Those guys in the Cobras might think they have matters under control, but it won't take much for things to get ugly."

PAKISTAN AIR Commodore Naqvi Rafique had approached the confrontation at Indus Junction with high hopes. Here, he'd thought, would be an opportunity to show the U.S. and NATO that the Taliban could be dealt with on his country's soil without civilian casualties. With help from neighboring tribesmen, he was certain that the Taliban warriors who'd been harbored in Balqhat could be quickly and decisively dealt with, and when he'd arrived at the intersection moments after the truck caravan had been brought to a stop, he could taste victory. In the back of his mind, he saw a chance to become only the second PAF officer to receive the Nishan-e-Haider—

Pakistan's highest military honor. It was an award that would propel him through the ranks and serve as a springboard for his political aspirations.

Everything had changed, however, once he saw women and children herded out of the lead truck and forced to encircle the caravan. In an instant, he'd found himself faced with the same dilemma allied forces had been faced with since day one of Operation Freedom—how to contend with the Taliban without putting innocent lives at risk.

Now, as he sat at the controls of the middle Cobra, watching the Kiowa and Black Hawk retreat into the clouds massed over the border, Rafique was torn with uncertainty. Gone was the option of using brute force to resolve the situation. Unleashing the Cobra's Hellfire missiles would likely kill the women and children as well as anyone in the trucks. Leaving things in the hands of the tribesmen also seemed inadvisable, as there was no guarantee they had any qualms about collateral damage. Short of abandoning the mission, there seemed only one other course.

"Take aim at the lead truck," he told his copilot. "Target the front windshields. Guns only."

As the copilot followed his orders, Rafique commanded the other two choppers to draw a bead on the second and third trucks, adding, "If we draw any Taliban out into the open, go after them, but I want those hostages kept out of the line of fire!"

The three choppers slowly pivoted, giving each gunner a chance to bring his three-barreled M197 into play. Each gun carried 750 20 mm rounds and was capable of firing more than a round per second. With a little luck, Rafique figured they could quickly take out the men riding up front in all three trucks. That alone wouldn't be enough to win the day, but it would buy the Pakistanis enough time to fly in closer and deal with any response from the survivors. And there would be a response—of that Rafique was certain. As long as one of them was still alive, he knew the Taliban would never surrender.

TALIBAN FIGHTER Yama Taher was thankful for the drone
of the helicopters overhead. It enabled him to crawl his way
up through the brush without concern that a light snapping
of twigs would betray his position. He wasn't alone. Three
colleagues were close behind him, slowly advancing on the
nearest group of Rodir tribesmen gathered halfway up the
hill from the road where the fleeing Taliban fighters had been
forced to a halt. He wasn't surprised that the Rodir had been
responsible for the spike strip. After all, what better way to
spite their rivals in Balqhat than to strike at the guests they'd
harbored all these months. No doubt there was some bounty
involved, too. The cowards were likely intent on blood money
even though they'd brought in the military rather than acting
on their own.

No matter, Taher thought to himself. If at least one of the
retreating U.S. choppers headed up to Balqhat, his mission
would already be a success. Now he and his men would ice
the cake by giving the Rodir and their airborne counterparts
their much-deserved comeuppance.

The flares had begun to die out by the time Taher's men
were within twenty yards of the enemy, but the Taliban leader
could still see the silhouettes of the Rodir. They seemed preoc-
cupied with the situation down on the roadway. That would
only make things easier.

All four of the terrorists had Kalashnikovs slung over
their shoulders. Taher was additionally armed with an RPG-7
launcher, and two rockets. While his men were dispensing with
the Rodir, he would direct a first shot at one of the Cobras,
then follow up by sending a second warhead into the middle
of the two trucks stalled on the highway. That vehicle was
packed with enough explosives to create a small Armageddon
at the highway junction. Yes, it would mean killing a few of
his own men along with the women and children, but it would
render the road inoperable, leaving the Rodir with no way
out of their hillside village. Once the fighting was done here,

it would make it that much easier for tribal warriors from Balqhat to sweep down and lay the homes of their neighboring opponents to waste once and for all.

ONCE HE'D RISEN above the cloud line, Grimaldi curtailed his retreat and swung the Kiowa Warrior around so that it was once again facing the Indus Highway intersection, more than a mile to the east. A hundred yards away, Kitt's Black Hawk had reversed its course, as well. Both choppers hovered in place as those on board stared pensively through gaps in the clouds, trying to determine how the confrontation below was playing out.

"Let's just hope they don't catch a glimpse of us and decide to take some long-distance target practice," Grimaldi told Bolan.

"I think we're an afterthought at this point," Bolan replied.

"That'll change if we head back."

"If we're needed, that'll have to be an acceptable risk."

"I'm with you," Grimaldi said. "But we can't even see the hostages. How do we tell if we're needed?"

Before Bolan could respond, a loud explosion ripped through the night air and the two men saw a distant ball of flame much like the one created earlier when the Apache had been shot down over the Safed Koh Range. Judging from the altitude, Bolan knew one of the Cobras had just been hit.

"I think that's our cue," he told Grimaldi.

15

The village tribesmen closest to Yama Taher's men heard the rocket launcher being fired well before its warhead struck one of the Cobras. They turned toward the noise and shifted aim with their own weapons, but by then a flurry of AK-47 rounds was tearing into them with deadly precision. Of the fourteen men caught in the Taliban's sights, all but one were brought down in a matter of seconds. The lone survivor dropped to the ground, using his fallen comrades for cover as he leveled his Kalashnikov and let loose with a fusillade of his own. Fellow tribesmen farther up the hill backed him up, directing their fire at the unseen assailants.

Two of Taher's men were riddled with kill shots, and the third was taken out of the fight with multiple wounds to his upper torso. Taher had been grazed as well but managed to dive into a scalloped culvert, taking him out of the line of fire. He'd abandoned the rocket launcher but still had his assault rifle. For the moment, however, he decided it was best to hold his fire and play possum. With all the ensuing chaos, there was a chance the tribesmen would hold off coming downhill to make sure they'd finished off their assailants. If they could be distracted, Taher figured he might yet live to fight another day. And with the RPG-7 still well within reach, he held out hope that he would have an opportunity to retrieve it and follow through on his plan to obliterate the truck caravan.

"STAY WITH THE PLAN!" Commodore Rafique shouted to his gunner, at the same time relaying the command on his headset to the men in the other Cobra. Below him, scattered across the Indus Highway, the burning remains of the downed chopper gave off ghostlike tendrils of smoke.

Moments later, his gunship's M197 rattled to life, pounding the lead truck with pinpoint accuracy. The vehicle's front windshield shattered, and the compartment turned red with the blood of the two Taliban gunmen inside. The same fate soon befell those in the second truck. The latter vehicle's transmission was in neutral, and when the slain driver's foot slid off the brake, the truck began to roll downhill, its flattened tires groaning. The women and children standing in the way screamed and barely managed to run clear before the truck rear-ended the lead vehicle and ground to a stop.

Seized with panic, the other hostages had already begun to flee in several directions, but when bullets streaked out of the brush toward them, one of the older women took control and shouted for everyone to double back and crawl beneath the two front trucks. In hopes of protecting them, she set down her ten-month-old son and snatched up an AK-47 dropped by one of the slain drivers. Squatting low to shield her child, she fired into the brush. Behind her, the others followed her command and flattened themselves once they reached the trucks, worming their way beneath the chassis. Before she could rejoin them, the woman was struck by two slugs from Taliban gunners. She slumped to the ground, mortally wounded, but somehow found the strength to drag her bawling son to where one of the other women could reach out and pull him to safety.

Rafique was mesmerized by the woman's dying gesture, but when he detected movement near the rear truck, he looked away and spotted a Taliban fighter hastily dragging the spike strip clear of the road. Behind him, the truck, its tires still intact, had begun to slowly back away from the vehicles in front of it. Once he'd finished, the terrorist paused long enough to fire his Kalashnikov at village tribesmen up in the surrounding hills, then bolted back toward the truck and quickly clambered into the front seat. By then the driver had pulled back a good twenty yards, giving himself enough room to hopefully squeeze past the stalled vehicles.

"They're going to try to make a run for it!" Rafique shouted, pointing at the truck. "Stop them!"

"Yes, sir!" the copilot shouted back.

Before the gunner could draw aim, however, the commodore saw a hail of incoming rounds obliterate the truck's windshield and ravage the two Taliban fighters in the front seat. Both men were killed instantly, the driver's slumped body sounding the truck's horn. At first Rafique thought the shots had come from tribal snipers up in the hills, but as he diverted his gaze, he saw two familiar helicopters swoop down from the clouds and realized the Kiowa had just weighed in with its pod gun.

"The Americans," Rafique whispered. Earlier, he'd spoken down to those in the Black Hawk in a voice heavy with disdain. Now, his words carried, if anything, a sense of relief.

"NICE SHOT," Grimaldi told Bolan as he continued to lower the Kiowa toward the roadway. Kitt's Black Hawk was close behind.

Bolan ignored the compliment and yanked off his headset. There was still more to be done. "Get me as close to the ground as you can."

"Will do," Grimaldi said. "Looks like we're catching a break on the diversion front."

Up in the surrounding hills, the surviving village tribesmen had tossed fresh flares into the brush-strewed slopes on either side of the road. The vegetation was too damp to ignite, but sudden illumination was bright enough to expose the handful of Taliban gunners who had been firing at the trucks. While the tribesmen drew their fresh targets into a firefight, the Cobras raked the hillside with searchlights and turned their M197s on another exposed group of terrorists.

The shift in the action gave the U.S. chopper crews a much-needed window of opportunity to reach the surviving hostages. Once Grimaldi had brought the Kiowa to within a few yards of the road, Bolan leaped to the shoulder, landing twenty feet in front of the lead truck. The Black Hawk, meanwhile, touched down farther uphill, just behind the rear vehicle. Kitt bounded out along with three of his men, then the chopper lofted back into the air, with the remaining commandos poised before the open doorway, carbines in hand, prepared to fire at anyone attempting to foil the rescue.

As he jogged past the trucks, Bolan crouched over and gestured to the women and children.

"Come with me!" he urged them.

The hostages remained in place, fear-stricken, eyes filled with terror. One of Kitt's men rushed forward and repeated Bolan's command in their native language, assuring them they would be taken to safety. Warily, the captives began to crawl out into the open. The young son of the slain woman screamed in the arms of the hostage carrying him, arms held out toward his mother. While Kitt and his men quickly flanked him, Bolan bent over and carefully picked up the woman's body. The boy was appeased but continued to sob as he and the other hostages were led back to the third truck. As one of the Taliban gunmen fired their way from the brush, he was met with a volley of shots from Kitt's men and quickly brought down.

The rear truck had rolled into the disabled trucks in front of it, but there was little damage to its front end. Bolan circled around and set the woman's body on the rear bed, then jogged back up to the cab and threw the driver's door open. He dragged out the slain Taliban behind the wheel and quickly took his place. The engine had stalled out, but once Bolan keyed the ignition, it turned over.

"Hurry!" he shouted back to the others.

One of Kitt's men crawled up into the truck bed and pulled the slain woman to one side, then helped the other hostages

aboard. When everyone else was in the truck, Kitt rushed
forward and pulled the other slain Taliban from the cab and
climbed into the front seat next to Bolan, ignoring the blood,
viscera and pebblelike shards of broken glass.

"So far, so good," he told Bolan. "Let's get the hell out of
here!"

AFTER DROPPING OFF Bolan, Grimaldi joined the Black Hawk
and two Cobras in providing aerial support for the village
tribesmen as they took on the dwindling Taliban force in the
surrounding brush. The Taliban may have struck a decisive
first blow, but the tide of the battle had quickly changed.
Shrubs that had offered concealment in darkness provided
little cover once flares and searchlights had been thrown into
the mix, and Grimaldi, like the others, had little problem spotting targets and doling out the necessary firepower to whittle
away at the enemy.

Noticing Bolan drive around the disabled trucks, the Stony
Man pilot felt things were under control enough for him to
splinter off and help escort the rescue vehicle. It had already
been determined that Bolan would try to transport the hostages across the border into Afghanistan. At this point, it
looked as if the mission would be carried out.

As he banked the Kiowa to align himself with the Executioner's truck, Grimaldi passed over a drainage culvert that
ran downhill parallel to the mountain road. It was a timely
maneuver, providing him with a glimpse of Taher. The Taliban
leader, far removed from the shifted battlefield, had reclaimed
his RPG-7 and was taking aim at the rescue vehicle, which
continued to inch its way past the other two trucks.

"Nice try," Grimaldi whispered, nosing the Kiowa downward. He strafed the culvert with the chopper's pod gun, stitch-
ing Taher with enough rounds to foil his shot. The Taliban
managed to fire, but the rocket flew wide, exploding on impact

with the hillside far beyond its intended target. Taher died without realizing his failure, and his blood soon mingled with rainwater trickling down the culvert.

COMMODORE RAFIQUE's helicopter flew low over the roadway, and he scanned the surrounding hillsides for more Taliban. To his right, the other Cobra did the same. The shooting had stopped and, except for the persistent throb of the gunships' rotors, the battlefield had fallen silent. Some of the village tribesmen continued to search through the brush, carbines in hand, while others retreated to tend to wounded colleagues and count their dead.

It was over.

After making one final pass, Rafique pulled away from the intersection and peered westward through the Cobra's slanted windshield. He could barely make out the taillights of the truck carrying the rescued hostages, but the two escort choppers were clearly in view, floating side-by-side above the highway leading to the Afghan border. Moments later, he received a brief radio communication from the Black Hawk's pilot.

"You're welcome."

16

Spin Range, Nangarhar Province, Afghanistan

"I'm sorry," Nawid Pradhan told Torialaye Yung. "The drug they shot me with hasn't worn off yet and—"

"You keep saying that!" Yung snapped irritably, cutting off the transient. "If you're going to help, then help! I've had it with your excuses!"

The two men were poised before the low table in Aden Saleh's mountain. In front of them, Yung's notebook computer was linked to Captain O'Brien's smaller unit with a patch cable. For nearly two hours, a software program Yung had been developing over the past two years had usurped the smaller computer's keyboard controls and had been entering possible security codes, but thus far it had been a futile effort. Several thousand variants had been tried so far, and each one had received the same Access Denied message. Adding to Yung's exasperation was the field computer's built-in shutdown command—after every five unsuccessful tries, the smaller unit would power off, necessitating a time-consuming reboot. With countless millions of other codes yet to be tried, Yung knew there was little, if any, chance of stumbling on the combination that would give him access to the computer.

Pradhan had suggested several possible ways to at least bypass the shutdown command, but none of them had worked and he seemed at a loss when it came to tweaking Yung's software program in hopes of speeding up the code-selection process. In truth, Pradhan was downplaying his expertise to the same extent he exaggerated the lingering effects of the tranquilizer dart he'd been shot with hours earlier back in Kabul. The drug had worn off and Pradhan was clearheaded, albeit racked with hip pain and filled with dread about his fate as well as that of his wife. He felt that their chances of surviving this latest adversity were every bit as slim as the likelihood of cracking the access code to O'Brien's computer. Still, if there was any way he could atone for the foolish way he'd placed his trust in Shah, he was intent on pursuing it.

And Pradhan believed there *was* a way. At the weekly bazaars near the air base he'd worked on enough military computers to learn how many of their owners had chosen their security codes. He suspected the solution to accessing O'Brien's computer lay a few feet away, where, several minutes earlier, Saleh had set O'Brien's mended combat fatigues on a weathered divan along with the slain captain's personal effects. Pradhan needed to find a way to get to the divan without drawing suspicion. Until that opportunity presented itself, the Afghan was determined to do what he could to increase Yung's frustration in hopes it would give him some bargaining leverage should his theory bear fruit.

After yet another series of codes failed, the microcomputer again shut down. Yung cursed and fumbled for a cigarette as Pradhan patiently went about rebooting the unit. As he did so, the Kabul native uncrossed his legs and rose to his knees. Yung took little note of the maneuver, as he'd done the same thing earlier when one of his legs had cramped.

So far, so good, Pradhan thought to himself. Now all he had to do was to bait Yung.

"Where did they take the women and children?" he asked the Uzbekistan.

"It's none of your concern!" Yung shot back, blowing smoke in the man's face.

"My wife is with them," Pradhan replied evenly. "That makes it my concern."

"Show me you're the expert you claim to be, or you'll be a dead man and it won't matter where your wife is."

"You plan to kill me anyway!" Pradhan scoffed bitterly. "If you think I don't realize that, you're a bigger fool than I am for trying to help you!"

The provocation worked. Yung lashed out, backhanding the Afghan squarely below the chin. The blow was even more forceful than Pradhan anticipated, making it easier for him to convincingly reel to one side. As he fell, he brushed against the divan with enough force to tip it over, spilling O'Brien's belongings to the floor.

Yung yanked a Glock 9 mm pistol from his web holster and aimed it at Pradhan's forehead. "You're in a hurry to die, is that it?"

Pradhan had bit his lip when he was struck. He glared sullenly at Yung as he wiped a trail of blood from his chin. He was about to reply when the front door swung open and Aden Saleh charged in, followed by one of his armed minions.

"What's the problem?" he demanded.

"He's been nothing but an aggravation!" Yung complained, gesturing at Pradhan. "He's worthless!"

"Maybe I'm just used to working alone without someone breathing down my neck!" Pradhan countered.

"Not likely," Yung said.

"Enough!" Saleh snapped. "We have enough problems. I don't need this to deal with!"

"Get him out of here and there won't be a problem!" Yung said.

"I have a better idea," Saleh told the Uzbekistan. "We need to use the smaller helicopter, but the instrument panel still isn't lighting up. Why don't you go see if you can do a better job of fixing it this time."

"It's one of the circuit boards," Yung said. "We couldn't get our hands on a replacement so I had to make do with a retrofit."

"I didn't ask for an excuse," Saleh said. "Can you fix it or not?"

Yung glowered as he holstered his Glock. Pradhan grinned at him and taunted, "Now you know what you sound like."

Yung was about to retort but thought better of it. He got up from the table and grabbed a tool kit on his way out of the cabin. Once he'd left, Saleh turned to Pradhan.

"As for you," he said, "you have until he gets back to show some results."

"Or else what?" Pradhan asked.

"There are many ways for a man to die," Saleh responded coldly. "Not all of them are swift and painless."

The Taliban leader gestured for his subordinate to remain and stand guard over the prisoner, then headed out of the cabin. Pradhan waited until the door had closed, then made his way back to the table. An hour earlier, Saleh's ultimatum would have been tantamount to a death sentence, but now Pradhan had his hands on what he hoped would be the key to accessing O'Brien's computer. He wasn't sure how to best play out his hand should he succeed, but at least he had a glimmer of hope.

Returning to the table, Pradhan dropped back to his knees and hunched over the two computers, doing his best to ignore the throbbing in his arthritic hip. The soldier guarding him righted the divan and kicked aside O'Brien's belongings before sitting down. From his vantage point, the guard was in no position to see that Pradhan held, cupped in his left palm, the slain captain's dog tags. If his theory was correct, the access code to O'Brien's computer had been derived from some combination of the letters and numbers on the tags. All that remained was to run the information through Yung's software and hope for the best.

As Pradhan began to type in the necessary commands, it slowly dawned on him that with Yung gone he had other options at his disposal besides merely tapping into O'Brien's database. The more he thought about it, the more he realized that it was not the microcomputer, but rather Yung's notebook that offered him his best chance of eluding the fate laid out for him and finding his redemption.

"WHAT IF IT'S NOT TRUE?" Rashid said. "Pakistan's as capable of spreading disinformation as anyone else."

The Afghan general was standing with Faryad near the helipad next to the truck that had brought the Kabul refugees to Aden Saleh's compound. The driver's door was open, and the dashboard radio was broadcasting the latest headline news from Pakistan. The top story had been the rout of Taliban forces in a skirmish at Indus Junction.

"If it wasn't true, Saleh would have heard from his men by now," Faryad replied.

"I still can't believe it," Rashid complained. "How many more setbacks can we afford?"

"Not many," Faryad said.

"That caravan was just supposed to be a diversion," Rashid said. "The hostages were supposed to bring things to a stalemate. Without that, what we had planned in Balqhat loses its impact. Now we don't even know if the Americans will bother to go there!"

"That's a possibility," Faryad conceded. "That's why we're going ahead with a contingency plan."

"What are you talking about?" the general demanded.

"Once Shah arrives, he'll be flown to Balqhat wearing the uniform we took off the American who was brought here," Faryad explained. "He'll carry out a modified version of the plan masquerading as a U.S. soldier."

Rashid stared at Faryad, incredulous.

"When was all this decided?" he fumed.

"Saleh and I discussed it while you were down here trying to reach your colleagues," Faryad said calmly as he glanced over Rashid's shoulder. One of Saleh's men was approaching them from the direction of the quarry. Clutched in his right hand was a Ruger pistol. Faryad nodded imperceptibly, then went on, "Shah is better than any of us at imitating American accents. He'll be able to—"

"Never mind that!" Rashid interrupted. "I want to know why I wasn't consulted about any of this!"

"Come now, General," Faryad responded. "You're an astute man. Surely you must realize how you've been compromised to where you're no longer of any use to us."

Rashid's face flushed. Before he could vent his rage, however, the man behind him raised his Ruger to the base of the general's skull and pulled the trigger.

THE LABYRINTH of tunnels that had so well served the Taliban reached Saleh's compound by way of the large cave housing the leader's concealed helipad. It was through an opening deep in the cave that Shah finally completed the long underground trek from Kabul River. Sitting upright in the back of the ATV, Shah welcomed the fresh night air and drew in a deep breath as he was transported across the helipad. When he spotted Yung working on the instrument panel of the small Bell 206 LongRanger, Shah leaned past the medic and asked the driver to stop. Yung glanced up from his work inside the cockpit and greeted Shah with a dour smile.

"The hero arrives," he called out.

Shah ignored the man's sarcasm and said, "It was your help with the Predator that made the difference. You're as much a hero as anyone."

"Well, the victory parade will have to wait," Yung replied. "We may have succeeded at Bagram, but since then it's been nothing but setbacks."

"Are you sure?" Shah said. "While I was being brought here some of our men shot down an enemy gunship. That has to count for something."

"Weighed against everything else?" Yung shrugged. "Not so much."

"What's happened?"

Yung stopped his work and climbed down from the LongRanger. Shah stepped out of the ATV and the two men walked away from the others. Shah's jaw throbbed, and his entire body still ached from the beating it had taken during his escape from Bagram, but he was steady on his feet and had little problem keeping up with Yung. The technician quickly filled Shah in on what he'd just heard about the debacle at Indus Junction, then explained that the allied forces had severed communications with the ANA regarding the deployment of troops out of the air base.

"At this point we don't know if they suspect anyone but Rashid of being in collusion with us," he concluded.

"What about Rashid?" Shah asked.

"See for yourself," Yung said, pointing down the trail leading from the helipad to the quarry. Shah turned and saw Saleh and a Taliban fighter standing near the edge of the pit, holding a body between them.

"They killed him?"

Yung nodded. "Be glad you showed up a hero," he said.

As Shah watched, Rashid's corpse was unceremoniously flung over the side. He heard the body land and seconds later the snarl of the snow leopards echoed up out of the quarry. Shah was torn with misgivings as he listened to the creatures tearing into their nocturnal feast. He was indebted to Rashid for helping him infiltrate Bagram and had come to view the general as something of a mentor. To see how quickly the man had fallen from grace was sobering. Yung was right—Shah was fortunate he'd succeeded in his mission to execute Karimi back at the air base; otherwise he'd likely have been fed to the leopards, as well.

Shah was still staring toward the quarry when Saleh turned and spotted him, then started to make his way toward him.

"He's glad to see you on your feet," Yung told Shah, "because he wants to throw you right back into the fray."

"I'm ready," Shah insisted. "What does he want me to do?"

"You'll find out soon enough," Yung told him, smiling slyly.

THE MAN GUARDING Pradhan bolted from the divan when he heard Saleh's voice just outside the door to the cabin. Pradhan took advantage of the man's distraction, leaning over from the table long enough to drop O'Brien's dog tags atop his camo fatigues. The tags had served their purpose.

Pradhan had plotted a way to leverage what he'd accomplished with the computers, but when the door opened inward, the refugee's mind went blank for a moment as he was overcome with shock. Following Saleh and Faryad into the cabin was none other than Shah.

"You!" Overcome with rage, Pradhan lunged forward, only to have his way blocked by the guard. Restrained, he continued to rail at Shah. "I was counting on you and you turned your back on me!"

"It couldn't be helped," Shah told Pradhan, his voice tinged more with annoyance than remorse. "The situation changed."

"Traitor!"

"Think what you want," Shah said, "but consider this. If you'd been let on the base you'd likely be dead now instead of here."

"And this is better than being dead?"

"Silence!" Saleh shouted. "Both of you!"

Pradhan ignored the command, his eyes still trained on Shah. "Why did you do it? After what I did for your—"

The guard cut the Afghan off, slamming the butt of his Kalashnikov into the prisoner's midsection. Pradhan doubled over, the wind knocked from his lungs. Shah calmly stepped around him and snatched up O'Brien's heaped belongings. He took note of the mismatched fabric that had been used to replace the section of pant leg blown away when O'Brien had stepped on the land mine.

"This is going to look conspicuous," he told Saleh and Faryad.

"Not if we film you from the waist up," Saleh assured him. "You'll have your back turned as well, so your face won't appear, either. You just need to be sure to shout loud enough."

"Using one of your American accents," Faryad added.

Shah grinned, even though the gesture aggravated his jaw. Perfectly mimicking a Tennessee backwoods twang, he told Faryad, "No worries, good buddy. It'll be a slam dunk, gay-roan-teed."

"That will work," Faryad said. "Beforehand, though, you'll need to sound British."

"Not a problem, mate," Shah replied.

"I think that's close, but the reporter you'll be mimicking is from Manchester, not London."

"If he's still alive, I'll just need to hear him say a few words and I'll have it," Shah promised.

"Yes, he's alive," Eshaq said. "He won't be killed until the last minute, in case there's a forensics check on when he died."

"Smart thinking."

"What are you talking about?" Pradhan asked Saleh once he was able to speak again. "What are you planning to do with my wife and the others? I demand to know!"

"Demand to know?" Faryad snickered to Saleh. "He sounds like Rashid just before we put him out of his misery."

Saleh ignored the wisecrack and told Shah, "Put on the uniform, then go to the helipad. The chopper should be ready."

Shah took O'Brien's things to the far corner of the main room and began to change. It was no easy task and he winced with every movement.

Pradhan, meanwhile, had recovered his wits and decided it was time to implement his plan.

"You're flying him to Balqhat," he guessed, doing his best to stand clear of the two computers on the low table behind him.

"What makes you say that?" Faryad asked.

"I could see a glow from city lights to the east of here when we were being driven up," Pradhan went on. "I'm guessing we're near Jalalabad, which means it'll be only a short flight south to cross the border."

"You didn't answer my question," Faryad said. He turned to the guard, who shrugged and shook his head.

"I didn't tell him anything," the guard said.

"Walking here to the cabin I saw fields down below," Pradhan said. "There wasn't much moonlight, but it looked like you're planting something. Poppies, right? For the spring harvest? Is that why we were drugged and brought here? To help with the planting?"

"Enough!" Faryad snapped.

He turned to Saleh and demanded, "What did Rashid put in those darts? This idiot won't stop babbling!"

Saleh furrowed his brow. "He was coherent enough a few seconds ago."

"What confuses me," Pradhan went on, speaking as if he hadn't been interrupted, "is that if we're here to plant, why go to the bother of loading my wife and the others onto a helicopter? The fields are barely a hundred yards downhill. It makes no sense. You have to be taking them somewhere else. Are they being flown to Balqhat, too?"

"I said *enough!*" The SVR operative stepped forward and grabbed Pradhan by the collar of his newly bought shirt. "Just answer my question—why were you talking about Balqhat?"

"You're choking me," Pradhan said hoarsely, making it seem as if he could barely get the words out. Saleh let go of his collar, shoving him slightly. As he had with the guard earlier, Pradhan made use of the bullying, backpedaling a few steps and pretending to stumble into the table. He reached down as if to balance himself and sat on the table's edge, blocking the men's view of Yung's opened notebook computer. O'Brien's smaller field computer was now within easy reach.

"Maybe I heard something while I was on the truck, and not just about Balqhat," he told Faryad cagily. "Which reminds me, which one of you is the one they call Saleh?"

Faryad lost patience and yanked his Ruger from his waistband. As he took aim at Pradhan, the prisoner grabbed hold of O'Brien's field computer and held it over his chest.

"Go ahead and shoot him," Shah called out from across the room.

"Before you do," Pradhan calmly suggested to Faryad, "maybe you should take a closer look at the computer."

Faryad took a step closer and eyed the palm-size screen, which displayed the homepage for Bagram's 25th Infantry Division.

"You cracked the access code."

Pradhan nodded, then thumbed the power switch, turning off the computer.

"When you turn it back on," he said, "you'll be right back where you started. Needing the code. Now, are you really sure you want to pull the trigger?"

As Faryad and Saleh exchanged a look, Pradhan discreetly reached behind him, powering off Yung's computer. He figured he'd recorded enough information and didn't want to risk having the others discover the Web cam had been filming from the moment they'd walked in the door. While he bargained with his captors, he had to hope that the footage he'd just taken had not been an exercise in futility.

17

"Hadn't thought about it," Bolan told Grimaldi.

The Stony Man pilot had just caught up with the Executioner in the sleeping quarters at the CIA field station at Kabul International Airport. Bolan was stretched out on a cot. His boots were off, but he was still wearing the ankle brace he'd been fitted with earlier that morning. He glanced at the foot Grimaldi had asked about and turned it from side to side, feeling little more than a dull, manageable pain.

"Good to go," he said.

"Glad to hear it," Grimaldi said, plopping down on an adjacent cot. "Of course, you realize that if you were a racehorse they'd take you out and shoot you."

"There's something to be thankful for," Bolan said.

It had been a little over an hour since the men had returned to the base in the Kiowa Warrior. Shortly after they'd crossed the border, Captain Kitt had taken over the wheel of the Taliban getaway truck and driven the rescued hostages to Bagram, where they were being treated at the medical center while Army officials mulled over the best course of action in terms of returning them to their village. The Pakistan military had offered to assist in the matter and had also issued an official statement of gratitude for the Americans' part in resolving the standoff at Indus Junction. They were reporting forty-two slain Taliban, more than twice the casualties sustained by the village tribesmen, while their own losses had been restricted to the crew of the downed Cobra. Come morning, there were plans for Pakistan to send troops to Balqhat to investigate the villagers' part in harboring the insurgents.

"Who knows, maybe tonight was a turning point as far as getting them to do a better job of cleaning up their own backyard," Grimaldi mused.

"Time will tell," Bolan said.

"I know this might sound a little strange," Grimaldi said with a yawn, "but I almost felt put out that we weren't asked to chip in and make the run to Balqhat."

Bolan nodded. "It feels like unfinished business."

The men fell silent. It didn't last long. Within a minute Grimaldi was asleep, his snores echoing through the room like the yawp of a chain saw. Moments later, there was a rap on the door. CIA agent Zane Anderson let himself in without waiting for an answer.

"Sorry to break up the slumber party," he drawled, "but you're not going to believe what we just came up with."

HALFWAY ACROSS THE WORLD, Brognola had just learned of the discovery, as well, and he was equally incredulous.

"Astounding," he said.

The SOG chief was standing beside Price, watching the video display Kurtzman had cued up on one of the monitors on the far wall. It was the second time they and the rest of the team had gathered in the Annex Computer Room and viewed Nawid Pradhan's Web-cam footage. They were still trying to digest the wealth of information the downtrodden transient had managed to disseminate in the video packet surreptitiously e-mailed to the owner of the Kabul cybercafé where he periodically worked. The communiqué had been relayed to local police and passed on to Army Intelligence at Bagram Air Base before coming to the Farm's attention, and Price had just learned that Bolan was reviewing the same footage at the CIA station located just outside the Afghan capital. Kurtzman had earlier run the footage through a transcriber program, allowing the group to read a printout translation of the exchange between those gathered with Pradhan in the darkened room.

Brognola felt the situation called for a fresh cigar. As he began to unwrap another of his expensive Padrons, he turned to the others, eager to map out a battle plan for dealing with the intel windfall.

"Okay, let's break it down, piece by piece," he said. "First off, the guy who sent this was apparently abducted somewhere near Kabul and taken to what I'm assuming is a Taliban safe house somewhere in the mountains near Jalalabad. There were others taken captive, as well, and from the sounds of it, they're headed for Balqhat by way of helicopter. Do I have all that right?"

Kurtzman nodded, glancing at his computer screen, which he'd broken down into several windows, one containing blown-up freeze frames in which Torialaye Yung's Web cam had captured images of four men, including the soldier guarding Pradhan. Pradhan's back had been to the camera throughout the video but, at this point, the Stony Man brain trust was more concerned with the identities of the others.

Once he'd transferred the screen with the facial shots onto another of the far wall monitors, Kurtzman addressed the group. "The man on the right's the one who saved us some work by tipping us off that he's Aden Saleh."

"The Taliban leader," Price said.

"The same," Kurtzman said. "I know we haven't done the deck-of-cards thing as far as they're concerned, but if we were, he'd be a face card, maybe even a king."

"I'd say you're right," Price said. "Most of the intel I've seen has him running most of the cross-border raids into Afghanistan."

"I'm sure he had a hand in what went down at Bagram, too," Brognola said. "But go on, Bear."

"On the left is our old friend Mehrab Shah," Kurtzman said, "clearly alive and well after his getaway. Given that

AI's reporting that someone accessed Captain O'Brien's field computer around the same time this video was made, I'd say it's a safe bet the computer's at the safe house and that it's his uniform Shah is changing into."

"The question is why?" said Delahunt.

"Before we get to that," Brognola said, "what about the other two men? Do we have a make on either of them yet?"

"Negative," Kurtzman said, "but Hunt's running their mugs through Profiler."

"Actually, I think we might have an ID on one of them," Wethers said, glancing at the data he'd been processing on his own computer. "Give me a moment."

The former cybernetics professor entered a few commands on his keyboard. Seconds later, a third screen on the far wall switched images to that of a man whose face Wethers's software had matched with Nawid Pradhan's second interrogator. The resemblance was undeniable.

"His name's Eshaq Faryad," Wethers reported, "and I hate to say it, but if he's in the mix it puts a whole new spin on things. He's from Uzbekistan, but the logs have him pegged as a longtime operative for Russian intelligence."

"Hey," Tokaido called out. "Another spin is right."

"Moscow working with the Taliban?" Brognola's fingers clenched his cigar. "That's the last thing we need."

"It fits, though," Price said. "The Istanbul conference is still a week off, but Russia's already calling for a vote to pull NATO troops out of Afghanistan. And they aren't alone."

The more Brognola pondered this latest development, the more he knew Price was right.

"If they're in collusion with the Taliban and can round up enough support for a pullout, the clock goes back twenty years and we're back to a Russian occupation."

"That's enough to keep you up nights," Delahunt said.

"And don't forget they've got ANA in their pocket on this, too," Kurtzman interjected. "Or at least some of them."

Brognola nodded. "General Rashid's name came up on the video," he said, "so it's pretty clear we were right about him. From the sounds of it, though, I don't see much chance we'll track him down alive."

"He can't have been working alone," Delahunt said. "Let's hope when ANA coughs up a few coconspirators."

"Let's leave that to them for now," Brognola said. "The way I see it, we've got two priorities—Balqhat and trying to locate the safe house this video was sent from."

"The tip-off coordinates are pretty broad," Kurtzman said, "but I think we can narrow down a search area on the hideout. Cloud cover's still a problem over there as far as sat cams go, but I can go through old feeds from the archives. If a planting field shows up with an adjacent helipad, we're golden."

"That'd be a break, all right," Brognola said, "but if something like that turned up it would've been flagged already, so don't get your hopes up. Any helipad's likely to be camouflaged or at least blocked from any sky views."

"I'll break out the fine-tooth comb," Kurtzman promised.

"Do that," Brognola said. "I'd also like somebody to go frame-by-frame through the video, focusing on the inside of the safe house. It looked pretty Spartan from what I saw, but maybe a closer look will turn up something."

"I'll take it," Delahunt volunteered.

"Good," Brognola said. "Now what about access routes? If those captives weren't helicoptered in, I'm thinking they had to come by truck. So let's also focus on cam shots of every roadway between Kabul and Jalalabad, especially ones that trail up into the mountains."

"Got it," Tokaido said.

"One other option," Kurtzman offered. "That Apache shot down while Striker was en route to Pakistan—he said it was brought down in the mountains pretty close to the area we're talking about. If there aren't any roads there, we've got to think in terms of tunnels."

"Good point," Price said. "And if Shah didn't get to the safe house by truck, there's a chance he came underground, too."

"We need to pull up a grid of all the tunnels we've taken out of commission in that vicinity," Brognola said. "Throw a wide net and figure wherever's there's a blank stretch, it's likely we missed something and'll have to lean on Bagram to make a more thorough sweep. Hunt, can you run with that?"

"Glad to," Wethers said.

"Okay, then," Brognola said. "That leaves Balqhat...."

"IT'S A GOOD THING AI was talked out of keeping this guy for interrogation," Bolan said. He was standing alongside Grimaldi and Zane Anderson in the latter's office, located directly above the service bay for the Agency's Kiowa Warrior. Before them, the last few seconds of Pradhan's secret Web-cam footage played out on Anderson's flat-screen computer monitor. "If they'd taken him into custody, we'd have never gotten this break."

"I never thought I'd say this," Grimaldi quipped, "but thank God for lawyers."

It was while viewing the exchange between Pradhan and Shah that Bolan had realized their benefactor was one of the demonstrators detained at the bazaar following the melee at Bagram. He'd overheard an Army Intelligence officer mention an Afghan who'd used Shah's name while trying to gain admission to the base just before the execution of Azzizhudin Karimi. This had to be the same man.

"Want me to play it back again?" Anderson asked. "I don't know about you, but I missed a few words here and there."

"Not right now," Bolan said, rustling the two sheets of paper in his hand. "Most of what we need is on the transcripts."

"There's a lot to run with."

"My people are looking into the whereabouts of this safe house," Bolan said. "I'm sure AI's doing the same."

"I'll put somebody on it here, too."

"What's the Army doing about Balqhat?" Grimaldi asked.

"Unless they've changed their minds since I last checked, nothing," Anderson confessed. "Pakistan's already said they're sending a team there in the morning, so Bagram's playing 'hands off.'"

Bolan quickly read over the portion of the transcript in which Shah and Saleh were discussing a plan that involved Shah wearing O'Brien's uniform and speaking in an American accent for some kind of video. There were no specifics and no timeline had been mentioned, but there had been a clear sense of urgency, and it had been equally clear that the plan likely involved the other prisoners Pradhan had referred to. Bolan didn't like the way it all added up.

"Tomorrow morning might be too late," he told Anderson.

"What can I say?" the CIA agent replied. "They think if we cross the border and start doing Pakistan's job for them again it'll muck up any points we just earned. Bagram wants them pulling their own weight."

"So we're supposed to sign off on a possible massacre just so Bagram can play politics?" Bolan shook his head. "I don't think so."

"You have a better idea?"

Bolan stared hard at Anderson. The CIA operative already knew what the Executioner had in mind. He stalled a moment, staring down at his copy of the transcript. Then, with a sigh, he leaned across his desk and keyed the intercom next to his computer, passing along a quick command to the mechanics in the service bay below.

"Get the bird ready to go back up."

18

Spin Range, Nangarhar Province, Afghanistan

The moment he returned to the mountain hut, Torialaye Yung charged past Aden Saleh and the Taliban soldier guarding Nawid Pradhan, who sat pensively on the divan near the two computers resting on the low table. The Uzbekistan technician grabbed Pradhan by the front of his shirt and pulled him to his feet, shaking him.

"You knew all along!" Yung shouted. "Admit it!"

Pradhan stared calmly at Yung and said nothing.

"Let him go!" Saleh told Yung, gesturing for the guard to intervene.

The guard stepped forward, placing a hand on Yung's shoulder. Yung jerked it away and continued to rail at Pradhan.

"There's no way you could have just stumbled onto that access code the minute I left!" he accused. "You had to have known it all along!"

"I told you to let him go!" Saleh commanded.

Yung relaxed his grip, then stepped back from Pradhan, but not before giving him a faint shove. The Afghan merely smiled.

"Everyone keeps grabbing at me and pushing me around," Pradhan responded whimsically. "Why is that?"

Yung turned to Saleh. "He knows more than he's letting on."

"He knows more than you about cracking security codes, I'll say that much," Saleh replied. "Find another way to vent your frustrations."

"I'll show you I'm right," Yung said. He knelt before the low table and turned on his notebook computer. "You'll see. I'll be able to track whatever he did."

"Perhaps not," Pradhan told him as he sat back on the divan.

Yung's computer began to boot up, then froze. The screen was blank except for a blinking cursor in the top left corner. Yung glared at Pradhan.

"What did you do?"

The man shrugged. "I'm not as smart as you think. I must have made some kind of mistake and disabled the computer."

Yung cursed and turned his attention to O'Brien's micro-computer. When he powered it on, the smaller unit booted its way to the same sign-in screen Yung had been unable to work his way past.

"Go ahead and try," Pradhan taunted. "Maybe you'll be lucky and *stumble* on the code."

Yung turned back to Saleh. "Why don't you force him to cooperate?"

"He'll cooperate," he replied. "In time. We've cut a deal."

"You bargained with him?" Yung was incredulous. "Why?"

"Why?" Saleh scoffed. "Because you failed."

"It's a trick," Yung protested. "I don't know how he managed it, but—"

"I don't want to hear it," Saleh interrupted. "Just tell me you managed to fix the helicopter. Were you at least that competent?"

Yung nodded irritably. "Yes, I fixed it," he said. "They've already taken off for Balqhat."

"I'm glad to hear it," Saleh said. "Now go take a walk until you can bring yourself under control."

Yung shot Pradhan an angry parting glance, then stormed out of the hut, slamming the door with so much force it extinguished half of the candles and fluttered the leopard skins draped across the windows. Saleh shook his head, then calmly relit the candles.

"I'm sure there's a chance he's right," he told Pradhan, "but I give you points for being shrewd. Who knows, if you continue to cooperate even after we've brought your wife back, there might be a place for you in our organization."

Pradhan did not answer immediately. He knew at this point he had few cards left to play. Yes, thus far, things had gone well for him. Though he'd been unable to barter for the release of all his fellow prisoners, at least he'd secured Saleh's assurance that his wife would be returned from Balqhat unharmed. In the end, he knew that might likely prove to be the only victory he achieved, but, for him, it would be the one that gave him the greatest consolation. He had no intention of joining the Taliban, much less following through on his promise to provide Saleh with access to the microcomputer once his wife was brought back to him. Pradhan knew that even if he were to cooperate, the Taliban would eventually kill both him and his wife. But at least this way there was a chance they would die together.

YOU MEAN EVERYTHING to me, Rob Kitt wrote beneath his signature at the bottom of the well-creased letter to his wife and children. It was the first time he'd added any text to the message since writing it so many months before.

Kitt refolded the letter and placed it back in his father's heirloom cigarette case, then slowly looked over the weathered photos he also kept in the container. Interacting with the hostages he'd helped rescue at Indus Junction had reminded the captain anew of just how much he missed his family, and he was thankful to have returned from yet another mission without his farewell letter having to be sent posthumously back to the States. He was just as grateful for the chance to serve his country and help ensure that his loved ones would never have to face the daily prospect of the sort of terror that had befallen the women and children used as pawns by the Taliban. He still found it hard to believe the terrorists could have stooped to such depths, and having witnessed it firsthand Kitt was determined, more than ever, to do all he could to see to their defeat.

After closing the case and slipping it back into his breast pocket, Kitt left his barracks at Bagram Air Base and walked past the ruins of the control tower and fuel depot to the administrative offices for Army Intelligence. He had a standing security clearance, and after exchanging a few words with the desk officer he passed through a security checkpoint and walked down the hall to a large work area partitioned into nearly two dozen cubicles. He stopped when he reached the one manned by Sergeant Stephanie Rijo, AI's Special Ops liaison officer. Rijo's only son had been killed a year earlier by a suicide bomber while serving in Iraq. Though Kitt was a few years older, he bore a vague resemblance to the young man and shared the same first name. Accordingly, in recent months Rijo had come to treat him almost as an adoptive mother. Having lost his parents years earlier, Kitt had welcomed the relationship. The fact that it often made him privy to AI's inner workings was only an added benefit.

"Any new developments?" Kitt asked once he and Rijo had exchanged greetings. They spoke quietly so as not to be overheard by the handful of other AI officials still working at this late hour in other cubicles.

"More than you'd think."

Rijo quickly related the news of Nawid Pradhan's breakthrough video e-mail, then followed up with the confirmation AI had received a few minutes earlier that a British reporter on assignment in Balqhat was reported missing after failing to check in for two successive conference calls scheduled with colleagues at the BBC.

Kitt, like Bolan had, pinpointed Pradhan as one of the Afghans detained following Mehrab Shah's escape from Bagram. Also like Bolan, his first instinct was that it was imperative to make a move on Balqhat, and he was irate over the Army's decision not to take action.

"We've notified Pakistan and stressed the urgency," Rijo assured Kitt. "Hopefully they've pushed up their timetable and have people on the way there as we speak."

"But there's no guarantee," Kitt said.

"No," Rijo confessed. "And before you get any ideas, I need to remind you that I've told you all this off the record. If you show up there, it's my head."

Kitt grinned at the woman. "You really know how to stop a guy in his tracks."

"There is a way you can help, though," Rijo told him.

"Name it."

"This Special Agent Cooper you've been working with. We're still not sure if he's with CIA, but he's very well connected," Rijo said. "Somehow his people got hold of the video and have already done some homework on trying to track down this safe house near Jalalabad."

"I'm not surprised," Kitt said. "Matter of fact, I'll lay you a side bet Cooper's probably on his way there already, if not to Balqhat."

"No bet," Rijo said. "But let me get back to what I was saying. His people have apparently been looking into tunnel systems in the mountains still being used by the Taliban. Their thinking is that whoever brought down that Apache we sent out earlier probably reached their firing position by way of tunnels running near this safe house."

"Makes sense," Kitt said. "We still don't know where it is, though?"

"Not yet," Rijo said, "but we have a couple choppers on standby. One's going to do aerial recon while the other goes to the crash site to retrieve the Apache crew and check for that tunnel. I'm thinking either assignment could wind up doing as much good for the cause as flying to Balqhat. If you want, you can take your pick."

"I'll take the tunnel."

Rijo smiled. "That's what my Robby would've done," she said. "It's more proactive."

Kitt smiled back, then said, "I was right, then."

"About what?"

"The reason Cooper's people fed us a lead on the tunnel is because he's not around to run with it," Kitt guessed. "That's gotta mean he's headed for Balqhat."

"DÉJÀ VU, EH?" Grimaldi said as he powered the Kiowa Warrior toward the Pakistan border.

"Something like that," Bolan replied.

For the second time that evening, the two men were flying over the Safed Koh mountain range where it had all begun the night before. Bolan found it hard to believe so little time had passed. It seemed as if days had passed since he'd been on the ridgeline with Howitzer O'Brien, listening to the Special Ops captain vent over the way the U.S. military had handled the war on terror in Iraq and Afghanistan. Staring down once more at that remote crest, Bolan felt renewed anger at the thought of O'Brien being riddled by sniper fire even as he was bleeding out from his bomb-severed leg. The Executioner was even more enraged by the notion that the Taliban had gone on to strip the man of his uniform in hopes they could somehow use it to cast shame on the country that uniform represented. Bolan planned to do everything in his power to avenge the blasphemy, and once he had his vengeance, he would track down the enemy safe house, where he was certain he'd find O'Brien's body.

"I keep trying to figure out what the Taliban's planning," Grimaldi said. "We know this Shah guy's ready to impersonate two different people, but that's it."

"I don't think the specifics are important right now," Bolan said. "It's enough to know they're planning to kill innocents and make it look like it was our doing."

"Not if we can help it," Grimaldi said.

"Let's just hope we get there in time," Bolan said.

19

Price had just finished speaking over the phone with Hal
Brognola, who'd returned to Washington for a meeting with
the President and Joint Chiefs of Staff. She hung up and rejoined her Stony Man colleagues on the other side of the
Computer Room.

"We've confronted Russia regarding Eshaq Faryad," she
told the others. "They're stonewalling."

"How so?" Delahunt asked.

"They're claiming he's been out of their intelligence loop
for years," Price said.

"Yeah, right."

"They also deny being party to any collusion with the Taliban," Price said. "They're saying their call for a NATO pullout
is just damage control. They think we should cut our losses
and let Afghanistan handle matters on their own."

"Based on ANA's track record the past few weeks?" Delahunt wondered. "Did we tell them those Taliban defeats were
all rigged?"

"Yes," Price said. "They were informed about Rashid acting
as a double agent, but insist it's beside the point."

"They're stonewalling, all right," Tokaido interjected. "If
you ask me, everybody else in NATO's going to see through
it and vote against the pullout."

"Let's hope you're right," Price said.

"As long as we're talking about ANA, I've just come up
with something," Kurtzman announced. He refilled his coffee

cup and rolled back to his workstation. On his computer screen was an intercepted dispatch between the Afghan National Army's Intelligence Branch and their Bagram counterparts.

"They found Rashid?" Price asked.

"No," Kurtzman said, as he skimmed through the intel. "But if he's already been taken out, this could be even bigger."

"They tracked down some of the other rotten apples," the mission controller ventured.

"Bingo," Kurtzman said. "I don't have anything on how they pulled it off, but they just raided a clandestine meeting of six ANA turncoats, including three other generals as high up the food chain as Rashid. There was apparently an attempt to destroy evidence, but enough was confiscated to point to clear collusion with the Taliban on all of those recent raids. Even better, one of the generals is already trying to cut a deal to save his neck."

"Nice," Delahunt said. "Nothing like a star witness and a little hard evidence to put down a mutiny."

"Bagram's followed up on the leads we fed them, too," Wethers piped in. "They've sent a team to check for tunnels near that downed Apache and have another chopper doing aerial recon for the safe house."

Price turned to Delahunt and Tokaido. "How are we doing on that front?"

"Nothing conclusive yet on the roadways," Tokaido reported.

"Ditto on the frame-by-frames," Delahunt said. "I'm trying to enhance things to bring up the lighting, but there's still not a whole lot to look at inside the safe house."

"Stay on it," Price said.

She turned to Kurtzman. "Any help from the eyes in the skies?"

"Let me check." Kurtzman switched tabs on his monitor, bringing up a series of sat-cam images culled from NSA databases. He skimmed through them and settled on two shots worth zooming in on.

"Okay," he said. "Still no helipads showing up, but I've got a couple prospects. First is an alpaca farm about five miles southwest of Jalalabad. I'm seeing what looks like a freshly planted poppy field, and there's an adjacent forest with a thick enough canopy to possibly conceal a helipad."

"Might be something there," Price mused, "but I'm thinking the alpaca angle's probably just a coincidence. What's the other one?"

"It's got a clear access road for starters," Kurtzman said, eyes trained on the second aerial shot. "And there's a wide path that leads past a poppy field and what looks like some kind of quarry before coming to a dead end at the base of a mountain."

"There was no mention of a quarry in Pradhan's video," Price said.

"I know," said Kurtzman, "but I'm thinking it might not be that visible at night so the guy might've missed it. It'll take some time, but I can try to get a thermal reading on that mountain to see if it turns out there might be some kind of cave or…wait, hold on a second."

"What is it?" Price asked.

"Hang on," Kurtzman said. He'd zoomed in on the quarry and was using an enhancement program to heighten the focus on what looked to be several animals roaming the base of the pit.

"I don't think this helps us any as far as the Taliban go," he said, "but if we were looking for poachers I'd say we hit the jackpot."

Price strode over to Kurtzman's workstation and stared over the analyst's shoulder at his computer screen.

"Snow leopards," the mission controller said.

"Going by the tails and their spotting, yeah, I think so," Kurtzman said. "I don't know what they're going for on the black market, but it's probably a good way to pull in some decent change between opium harvests."

Across the room, Delahunt had just looked through her own latest batch of enhanced zoom frames from Pradhan's videotape. She let out a shrill whistle and clapped her hands.

"Yes!" she cried out.

"Got something?" Price asked her.

"I think Bear might've just found our safe house."

"What'd you come up with?"

"I've got a brighter room to look at," Delahunt reported, "and guess what I'm seeing on those skins stretched across the windows? Spots!"

Mt. Balqhat, Federally Administered Tribal Area, Pakistan

GRIMALDI MADE A SINGLE, high-altitude pass over Balqhat before easing the Kiowa northward toward the sheer, lofty peak of the tallest mountain overlooking the remote village. There were only patches of snow on the south facing, but on the other side of the mountain a thick, white layer blanketed the entire slope. Not surprisingly, a portion of the incline had been groomed for skiing. Grimaldi brought the chopper in for a landing on a plow-cleared parking lot next to the small, rustic lodge Zane Anderson had pointed out on a topographical map before the Stony Man commandos had set out from Kabul. The parking lot was empty and the lodge was dark.

"Looks like he was right about it shutting down overnight," Grimaldi told Bolan, eyeing the darkened structure as he killed the Kiowa's engines. "Nobody pulling guard duty, either, from the looks of it."

Unfastening his seat belt, the Executioner grabbed an H&K MP-5 subgun fitted with a Raptor II sound suppressor. "Let's hope so," he said. "We're cutting it close enough as it is."

When they'd passed over the Taliban hideaway moments earlier, the Stony Man operatives had spotted a parked Huey chopper, but no signs of activity. Much as they would have preferred having the Kiowa's arsenal at their disposal, given the likelihood of a hostage situation, the men had decided, even before leaving the CIA facility, that it would be too risky to go in with the helicopter. It had to be a stealth mission and to carry it out, it would be necessary to find a quick way down the other side of the mountain without drawing attention. Given what sketchy information Anderson had been able to access on the ski lodge, there seemed a good chance that the facility would provide Bolan and Grimaldi with the equipment they'd be needing.

The lodge was as modest as it was small, and the men were able to quickly determine that the building wasn't rigged to an alarm system. Grimaldi tripped the front lock in less than ten seconds. There was no one inside to confront them once they crossed the threshold into the cramped lobby. Grimaldi directed the beam of his flashlight along the wall behind the main counter. There was ample supply of rental skis and related equipment, but it had already been determined that the south side of the mountain was too steep and barren of snow for the men to even consider attempting to ski their way down to the hideaway. They had another means of access in mind, and Grimaldi smiled when the flashlight's beam fell on a bin stocked with heavy rope, anchor pins, carabiners, climbing harnesses and other rappelling gear.

Bolan reached into the bin and grabbed a length of rope, gauging its strength. It would do. He glanced at Grimaldi and nodded.

"We're in business."

20

A row of small, green flags snapped in the cold mountain breeze on the Safed Koh ridge as Rob Kitt cleared the rise leading to the avalanche that had buried Arsalan Kali. The flags, inscribed with gold lettering, were tethered to a wooden pole rising up from the debris at the spot where Kali had met his fate, the man's body nowhere to be seen.

"They got to him already," Kitt told the five Special Ops commandos who'd accompanied him on the short uphill trek from where their Huey had touched down. Four other soldiers were still halfway down the slope, tending to the grim task of transferring the fallen Apache crew into body bags.

"What's with the flags?" one of the commandos asked.

"A tribute to the men who die fighting us," Kitt explained. He reached out and stilled one of the flags so the men could see the inscription. "I can't translate, but I'm sure it says something about 'martyrdom' and their 'noble cause.'"

"Seems like that applies more to the men we lost in the Apache," the commando responded.

"I don't think they see it that way." Kitt let go of the flag and reached to his waist. Clipped to his ammo belt, along with several grenades and a full-face gas mask, was a high-powered flashlight. He grabbed the light and shone its beam on the ground just to the right of the debris.

There were boot prints in the loose soil.

"I'm guessing they came up out the tunnel to get the body," Kitt theorized. "With any luck, these tracks'll lead us to the entrance."

Kitt thumbed off the safety on his 9 mm pistol and started following the tracks. The others followed close behind, clutching M-16s.

"This is too easy," one of them said. "They usually do a better job of covering their tracks."

"Maybe they didn't get a chance," Kitt reasoned. "We've been doing a lot of flyovers along this stretch."

"That could be it," the other soldier replied as he began to scan the surrounding mountainside. "Then again, maybe we're walking into a trap."

"That's crossed my mind."

Kitt recalled Special Agent Cooper's close call the previous night when he'd discovered the tunnel used by the Taliban force that had massacred the ops unit a few miles to the north. If the enemy was lying in wait for them underground, he had no intention of blundering into their crosshairs.

The tracks ended less than ten yards from the flagpole. There, amid displaced rubble from the landslide, sat a flattened boulder with roughly the same diameter as a manhole cover. Kitt directed his flashlight at the stone and could see that it had been recently moved.

"Here," he said, handing the light to the soldier closest to him. He holstered his pistol, then retrieved two grenades from his ammo belt. One was an M-84 flash-bang, and the other was filled with CS tear gas. He handed the M-84 to another of the soldiers, then tucked the tear-gas grenade under his armpit, leaving both hands free to don his gas mask. The other men quickly followed suit.

"If you can, just tilt the rock up instead of sliding it," he directed two of the men without the grenades. "Leave room so we can make a quick toss into the opening."

"Got it."

Kitt readied his grenade as the two soldiers crouched on either side of the boulder, clawing their fingers into the dirt around it. Once they had a sufficient grip they tipped the rock up at an angle, exposing the tunnel entrance. Kitt quickly tossed the gas grenade down the opening. The other soldier did the same with the M-84. When it detonated, enough concussive force shot back up the opening to knock the boulder from the hands of the men holding it. Tear gas began to waft upward, but before it could obscure his view, Kitt caught a glimpse of the ladder rungs imbedded in one side of the vertical shaft. Drawing his pistol, the captain took it upon himself to lead the charge underground.

"Follow me!" he commanded.

One by one, the commandos lowered themselves down the gas-shrouded orifice. Even before he reached the base of the shaft, Kitt heard cursing and retching. Once he reached the bottom of the ladder, he dropped to a crouch, then pushed away from the rungs, rolling across the cold ground floor of the subterranean checkpoint. A gunman fired wildly in his direction, gouging the rocks just above Kitt's head. The captain spotted his would-be assailant through the thickening haze and returned fire, dropping the Taliban gunner. There were three other terrorists in the chamber, but they were too disoriented and nauseous to offer much resistance. Kitt killed one of them as he was trying to take aim with his AK-47, and the other commandos made quick work of the remaining two before they could clamber aboard the ATV one of them had just driven back from Saleh's compound.

Rising to his feet, Kitt joined his fellow soldiers and quickly checked to confirm the enemy had been neutralized. The tear gas had already begun to dissipate, and once they'd checked the bodies, the commandos surveyed the rest of the chamber, coming across the ammo cache as well as the underground phone.

"Nice little setup," one of the soldiers shouted through his mask.

"I'm guessing there are more places like this all through the mountains," Kitt said.

Another of the commandos raised a tarp laid across the back of the ATV and called out, "This must be their 'martyr.'"

Kitt joined the soldier and nodded as he stared down at Kali's bruised corpse. Shifting his gaze, he took note of the tire tracks on the ground.

"They just turned this thing around," he said. "You gotta think they were planning to take the body back to the safe house."

"Sounds right to me."

Kitt turned to the others. "Let's get the body out, then everybody on board. Grab a couple of those rocket launchers, while you're at it. Before this is over we just might need 'em."

21

Balqhat, Federally Administered Tribal Area, Pakistan

While neighboring Parachinar was a large, bustling city intent on making strides toward modernization, Balqhat had foregone such amenities in favor of the agrarian simplicity of another era. The village was comprised almost entirely of small farms separated by natural boundaries, and were scattered around a sparse market square. At this late hour the square was shut down, and the farms were all dark except for one. Set back at the edge of town on a raised knoll thick with trees and dormant grass, the smallest of Balqhat's five alpaca farms was flanked east and west by towering pines. It was nestled against the mountains, where a year-round snowcap fed a steep waterfall that, in turn, gave life to several creeks that meandered through the eight-acre property. There were lights on in the farmhouse, as well as in one of two larger outbuildings. The alpacas were bedded down for the night in the darkened barn along with a menagerie of goats, pigs and domesticated geese. Next to the other building, Saleh's Bell LongRanger had just touched down alongside the Huey that, hours before, had left the terrorists' compound in Afghanistan filled with the hostages seized from the caves outside Kabul.

Once they'd disembarked from the chopper, Faryad and Shah strode past the Huey and a piled heap of denuded grapevines and tree branches picked clean in recent weeks by the goats. As the two men approached, a rifle-toting sentry posted outside the building stepped to one side and held the door open.

"Is everything ready?" Faryad asked, his breath frosting in the cold night air.

The sentry nodded. "A helicopter passed by a while ago but went over the mountain and hasn't returned."

"It's probably nothing," Faryad said. "Still, we should move fast. Go ahead and douse the kindling."

Set beside the sentry was a five-gallon container already filled with gasoline. As he carried it over to the woodpile, Faryad and Shah entered the two-story building, which had been originally intended for storage but for the past few months had served as a temporary barracks for ever-shifting numbers of Taliban. For the moment, the structure served as a holding area for the Kabul hostages, who, except for two young children, were gagged and bound together in one corner, watched over by three more armed men. In addition to those from Kabul, there was another prisoner, Brooks Rufferts, a middle-aged television journalist for the BBC who'd made the untimely mistake of coming to Balqhat to do a story on the village's alpaca industry. He'd been taken captive by the Taliban two days earlier and accused of being a spy for NATO Intelligence. The journalist vehemently denied the charge during the course of a protracted interrogation that had involved makeshift waterboarding at the base of the waterfalls. Plans to videotape Rufferts's execution with his own camera had been put on hold when the Taliban learned that AI had pinpointed Balqhat as one of their safe havens in Pakistan. It had been Faryad who'd proposed that the camera could be put to better use. Now, he was ready to carry out the alternative plan.

Shah followed close behind as the SVR agent approached the prisoners. Pradhan had provided a description of his wife, and once Faryad picked her out of the group, he untethered her binds and pried free the duct tape across her mouth. After pulling her to her feet, he told one of the guards, "Take her to the Huey and start the engine."

"Where are you taking me?" the woman asked.

"To your husband," Faryad told her. "We are not without compassion."

"What about the others?"

"You would be wise to count your blessings and not to ask so many questions," Faryad replied.

As the woman was led out, Faryad turned his attention to Rufferts, a stocky, jowl-faced man with a pencil-thin moustache. He untied the rope around the man's ankles but left his hands bound and kept the tape across his mouth. The reporter's eyes were filled with a combination of fear and resignation.

"You're coming with us," Faryad told him.

Shah pulled Rufferts to his feet and escorted him from the building. Faryad remained a moment to confer with the guards. They spoke in whispers, well beyond earshot of the hostages.

"The door will be left open," Faryad explained. "When you see flames, untie the prisoners and remove their gags, then leave out the back way as fast as you can."

"Understood," one of the guards said.

"What happens to them?" another queried, gesturing at the female hostages.

"It's up to them," Faryad said. "The first to leave will be shot. The missile will take care of anyone who stays behind."

"How will we make it look like the Americans are responsible?"

"Leave that to us," Faryad said.

The SVR agent went to a storage rack and removed a sophisticated Minicam etched with the initials *BBC,* then left the building and joined Shah and the journalist near the woodpile. The sentry was still splashing gasoline on the cluster of vines and branches.

"Keep an eye on the prisoner," Faryad told him.

The guard emptied the gas can, then tossed it aside and turned his attention to Rufferts as Faryad took Shah aside, anxious to make certain the younger man understood the plan.

"You know what you're supposed to do?"

Shah nodded. "Once the fire starts, I start filming and give a play-by-play."

"Just enough to give a sense that our friend here is doing the reporting."

"I need to hear him speak so I can imitate him."

"In a moment," Faryad said. "Be sure you mention BBC right from the start."

"Of course," Shah said. "And after I've done a little reporting, I'll hand off the camera and double around the fire so that I can start shooting when the prisoners come out."

"Making sure to keep your back to the camera," Faryad reminded him. "And shout loud enough that it'll be picked up."

"I understand." Shah switched to his Tennessee accent and practiced his lines. "I don't care! Kill them all!"

Faryad smiled. "That should work. They'll be able to see that it's women and children you're gunning down."

"But I don't charge the building if only a couple of them come out."

"Correct," Faryad said. "All you need to do is establish we're killing innocents in cold blood. I'll be up in the chopper to launch the missile and finish things off."

"And by morning the videotape finds its way to Al Jazeera."

Faryad nodded. "For once, there'll be no way for the U.S. to claim civilians were merely collateral damage. It will look as if they've been caught red-handed, and by the time they start putting out denials, everyone's minds will have already been made up."

"Beautiful," Shah said.

Faryad removed a cigarette lighter from his pocket and thumbed it to life as he approached the woodpile. He squatted long enough to set fire to the kindling, then stepped back as the flames quickly began to spread. Gesturing to Shah, he rejoined the captive journalist and tore free the man's gag.

"You have one more chance," he told the prisoner. "Confess that you're a spy and give us the details."

"I've already told you," Rufferts protested. "I'm a documentary reporter, nothing more. I swear it on my mother's grave."

"Thank you," Faryad said. "That's all we need to hear."

The journalist looked confused. Faryad turned to Shah, who nodded, then proceeded to repeat Rufferts's words, perfectly mimicking the man's Manchester accent. "I've already told you. I'm a reporter, nothing more. I swear it on my mother's grave."

"What's the meaning of this?" Rufferts wanted to know.

Faryad smiled as he withdrew his Ruger pistol.

"You're about to film a far more important documentary than one having to do with alpaca farming," the SVR agent explained, raising the gun and aiming it at the reporter's forehead. "Unfortunately, it won't actually be you who's doing the reporting."

Faryad was about to pull the trigger when a quick series of muffled shots sounded from the side of the barn that housed the farm animals. The SVR agent howled and staggered into the sentry, blood erupting from bullet wounds in his upper torso. The guard grabbed for Faryad as the man's legs gave out. Shah, meanwhile, looked around wildly. The growing bonfire threw off enough light for him to spot Bolan charging clear of the barn, clutching his silencer-equipped MP-5.

The sentry saw Bolan as well and let Faryad drop to the ground. He whirled and was about to return fire when the Executioner triggered another burst of 10 mm slugs. The rounds tore into the sentry with lethal force, killing him.

"You!" Shah cried out, recognizing the man he'd nearly run over back at Bagram Air Base. He cast aside the video camera and bent over, grabbing for the SVR operative's fallen pistol. Rufferts intervened, kicking the weapon aside, then tackling Shah to the ground. They struggled briefly before Shah gained a quick upper hand and broke free. He dazed the reporter with an elbow jab to the side of the head. Cursing, Shah reached out and snatched up Faryad's gun.

"I wouldn't try that if I were you," Bolan warned Shah. He'd reached the bonfire and stood only a few yards away from the renegade.

Shah glared at Bolan and raised the pistol into firing position, forcing the Executioner to empty his MP-5. Shah was propelled backward by the rounds. He groaned as he crumpled alongside Faryad, adding fresh crimson splotches to O'Brien's already bloodstained uniform. In the flickering light of the bonfire, Bolan could see where the fatigues had been hastily patched in hopes of better allowing Shah to masquerade as a U.S. soldier.

"Where's the man you took this uniform from?" Bolan demanded as he crouched over his victim.

"In the place you call hell," Shah spit weakly, his eyes filled with hate.

"You'll be there before he ever will," Bolan assured the traitor.

Blood gurgled up through Shah's lips as he expended his final breath invoking a dire prediction.

"You'll never defeat us!"

The Executioner stared coldly as the life faded from Shah's eyes. The dead man continued to look at Bolan, as if to taunt him from the Great Beyond.

"We'll never stop trying," Bolan vowed.

ONCE THEY'D RAPPELLED down the mountain, Grimaldi had split off from Bolan, and by the time the Executioner was forced to make his presence known, the Stony Man pilot had stolen his way across the grounds to within a few yards of the idling Huey. The soldier who'd ushered Pradhan's wife into the rear compartment was up front at the controls. He was distracted by the activity near the bonfire and didn't hear Grimaldi's approach until the flyboy had yanked open the cockpit door. When he turned toward the noise, the soldier was struck squarely in the jaw with the butt of Grimaldi's MP-5. The man went limp. Grimaldi climbed into the cockpit and wrestled the man from the pilot's seat, then quickly dragged him into the rear compartment, where Pradhan's wife watched on with horror. She'd been struck in the face and her blouse was torn, forcing her to clasp at it to cover herself.

"I need your help," Grimaldi told the woman. When she stared at him, uncomprehending, he retrieved an AK-47 from the cockpit floor and held it out to her while pointing at the still-unconscious soldier. "Keep an eye on him. Do you understand?"

The woman grasped the weapon tentatively at first, then steadied her hands and calmly aimed it at the soldier's head. She pulled the trigger once and stared at the carnage the Kalashnikov had wrought, then looked up at Grimaldi.

"My English is poor," she told him, her voice hard. "You said I should kill him if he tried to force himself on me, yes?"

Grimaldi wasn't about to pass judgment. He was also certain that the woman's English was better than poor.

"The other hostages," he said. "They're in the building you just came out of?"

The woman nodded. "There are more soldiers with them."

"I'll do what I can," Grimaldi said, pointing at the building. "If they come out before I can get to them, do what you have to."

The woman nodded, taking aim out the open doorway with the AK-47.

"Go," she told Grimaldi.

THE TALIBAN GUARDS inside the makeshift barracks had followed orders and begun to unbind the hostages as soon as they saw the first glimmer of flames from the bonfire. Now, having just heard the report of an assault rifle, they assumed that the BBC journalist had been executed and that everything was going according to plan. They quickly freed the last few hostages, then pointed to the open doorway.

"That way!" one of the soldiers commanded. "Now!"

The hostages stared at the carbines directed their way and began to comply, taking slow steps toward the doorway. When several of the women stopped to gather up their children, another of the soldiers lost his patience and fired a round over their heads, shouting, "Faster! Or would you rather die in here?"

The children began to wail. The women hastened their steps, some sobbing, others mute with fear. By the time they'd reached the opening, their guards had already begun to rush toward a second, smaller doorway at the rear of the building. The first one to reach the door threw it open and charged out into the night. The others quickly followed. The last man to leave paused for a moment to glance back at the prisoners, who were completing their own exodus. His understanding was that they would be shot the moment they left, yet the only sounds he could hear were the crackling of the bonfire and the idling drone of the Huey, which was supposed to have taken off already to facilitate the bombing of the safe house.

"Something's not right!" he cried out as he caught up with the others.

But they had no time to respond. They'd just circled the rear of the building and stopped cold in their tracks when they saw Grimaldi standing alongside the building twenty yards from them, MP-5 raised and aimed.

"Surrender!" he yelled.

One of the soldiers was quick to comply. The others, however, refused to back down and were raising their weapons when Grimaldi unleashed a lethal zigzag of autofire. One of the terrorists managed to get off a wild shot that scarred the side of the building, but the others went down without firing. The man who'd surrendered had been caught in the line of fire and dropped to one knee, a bullet lodged in his right thigh. He'd already cast aside his AK-47, and as Grimaldi cautiously approached, he was quick to clasp his hands atop his head. Grimaldi kept his subgun trained on the man as he checked the others to make sure they were dead. Then he grabbed the survivor by one arm and jerked him to his feet. The man screamed in pain as he was forced to put his full weight on his wounded leg.

"Sorry about that," Grimaldi told him. "War is hell."

The Stony Man pilot escorted his prisoner back toward the bonfire. There, Bolan was busy rounding up the bewildered hostages. The BBC reporter had shaken off his fear and let his documentarian instincts kick in. Video camera in hand, he was filming the aftermath of the rescue, complete with personal commentary that understandably ramped up the drama of the ordeal he'd just barely managed to survive.

"Got a keeper," Grimaldi told Bolan. "If somebody'll act as interpreter, maybe we can find out what was supposed to happen here."

Bolan gestured toward the Huey, where Pradhan's wife stood vigilant in the rear compartment doorway, Kalashnikov in hand.

"Stay by the helicopter," he told the hostages. "We'll make sure you get home."

While the women and children made their way toward the Huey, Bolan veered off and circled back around the bonfire to where Faryad lay next to Shah. Grimaldi joined him. Rufferts was close on his heels, camera rolling. Bolan shook his head and reached out, cupping one hand over the camera's lens.

"No footage showing our faces," he warned the reporter. "Just say we're part of the American Special Ops force and leave it at that. Understood?"

"I already have you on film," Rufferts confessed. "The whole rescue of the hostages as they were coming out of—"

"Delete it!" Bolan interrupted.

"But I have an obligation as a reporter to—"

"Right now you have an obligation to the people who just saved your neck," Bolan told the man. "Lose the footage!"

The reporter seemed disappointed but nodded. He was about to check the playback on his viewfinder when Bolan stopped him.

"First get some quick face shots of these two," he said, indicating Shah and Faryad. "Do it in such a way that it's clear they were here. When you're finished, we need to strip off one of them to get back a uniform belonging to one of our men killed back in Afghanistan. None of that goes on film. Is that clear?"

"If you insist," Rufferts replied dourly.

"Listen up, sport," Grimaldi told the Briton. "You've got the kind of scoop careers are made of. Quit your pouting."

"Who are you, anyway?" the reporter asked.

"If you put anything out there that could possibly identify us, we'll be your worst enemy," Grimaldi said.

The reporter fell silent. Once Bolan let go of the camera, Rufferts panned from the Huey past the bonfire to the bodies of Shah and Faryad, then zoomed in on each man's face. When he was finished, he left Bolan and Grimaldi and made his way back toward the hostages. Once they were sure they were off camera, Bolan and Grimaldi set to the task of stripping Shah of Howitzer O'Brien's uniform. They worked quickly and had finished the task when a mechanical growl sounded in the skies overhead. Glancing up, Bolan and Grimaldi spotted a pair of Pakistani Cobras approaching the farm.

"They're a little late," Grimaldi said.

Bolan raised his arms to get the attention of those in the choppers. Moments later, a searchlight shone down from the lead chopper, half-blinding him with its harsh glare. Bolan diverted his gaze and pointed toward the Huey, hoping the

Pakistanis would realize what had happened and hold their fire. The choppers hovered in place a moment, then slowly descended toward the farm. By the time they'd landed, the Stony Man warriors had circled back around the bonfire and were headed toward the Cobras. The first man out of the lead chopper was Naqvi Rafique. The commodore was poker-faced.

"I know this was supposed to be your affair," Bolan told the Pakistani, "but we were up against the clock. We had to act."

Rafique stared silently at the Executioner, then said, "I recognize you from earlier this evening. There's no need to apologize."

Bolan quickly related how the rescue effort had played out, concluding, "If you want to take over from here, that's fine." Indicating O'Brien's bloodied uniform, he added, "We have what we need."

Rafique nodded.

"You mentioned that your helicopter is across the mountain," the commodore said, flashing a faint grin. "It's not so easy to rappel uphill. Perhaps you'd like a ride."

22

Spin Range, Nangarhar Province, Afghanistan

Aden Saleh slammed down the receiver on the trunk line linking him with checkpoints along the Taliban's underground passageways. In his other hand he clutched a black-market cell phone that had similarly failed to put him in touch with those he was waiting to hear from.

"What's the matter?" Torialaye Yung called out from across the room. The Uzbekistan was seated at the low table, fighting his own frustrations as he tried to coax life back into his disabled laptop. His back was turned to Nawid Pradhan, who was now bound and gagged in the shadows, doing his best not to revel at the level of agitation weighing on his captors.

"They should have retrieved Kali's body by now," Saleh complained. "I was supposed to receive confirmation."

"Maybe they're still out on the mountain," suggested the guard standing watch over Pradhan. "They were going to place flags, remember?"

Saleh shrugged off the explanation and went on. "No one's responding in Balqhat, either. I need to know if things went as planned."

"You're being paranoid," Yung said. "Have a little patience."

Saleh scowled his way to the window and pulled aside the leopard skin, then leaned close to the glass and peered out into the night. There was little to see in the surrounding darkness. Still, the Taliban lieutenant felt a sense of dread, a premonition that things had somehow gone awry. He gave in to the feeling and as he strode quickly back to the main phone, he told the guard, "Go get up into one of the sniper posts in the trees."

The guard complied, letting in a cold draft as he headed out into the night. Saleh fought off an involuntary shiver and stabbed the cell phone's speed dialer. Instead of the check-point, he was calling the downhill barracks. He was relieved when someone picked up, but his nerves remained on edge.

"Douse all but one light in the barracks, then get the men out," Saleh ordered. "Stake out positions around the perimeter and be ready."

"Ready for what?" the soldier on the other end of the line wanted to know.

"Anything," Saleh advised. "Be ready for anything."

FORTY-FIVE MINUTES after commandeering the ATV, Kitt and his men finally emerged from the underground tunnels and found themselves at the rear of a large, cavernlike opening in the base of the mountain they'd just navigated their way up through. Before them, moonlight shone on a large, vacant helipad near the mouth of the cave. Just beyond the pad a large transport truck sat idle on a narrow dirt road.

"Looks like the place all right," one of the commandos whispered as Kitt shut off the ATV's engine.

As he climbed out of the cart, Kitt took a palm-size radio transceiver from his hip pocket. He'd been unable to make contact with the rest of the Huey crew since setting out from the subterranean checkpoint, and he quickly realized he couldn't pull in a signal within the cave.

"Let's recon, then I'll try again," he told the others as he stuffed the radio back in his pocket.

Kitt led two of his men around the northern periphery of the helipad while the others circled around from the other direction, converging moments later at the vacant truck. From their new vantage point, the men saw that the dirt road led down a steep incline to a field of freshly planted farmland that stretched to a hillside where a dim, flickering light shone from within a low, wide building camouflaged with a sod roof. A narrow path led northward to a much smaller hut surrounded by tall pines. Another light, equally faint, seeped through narrow seams in whatever was covering the windows. There was no sign of activity outside either structure.

"What's the chance we've caught 'em all napping?" one of Kitt's men whispered.

"I wouldn't count on it," Kitt said. "There's gotta be sentries posted somewhere. Stay on the alert."

There was no sign of the Huey, and though Kitt was able to raise a signal on his transceiver, the chopper was apparently too far out of range to pick it up. At least for the moment, he and his men were on their own.

"We'll take the hut," Kitt told the other team. "Go ahead and check out things downhill. Space out and be ready to use whatever cover you can find."

The soldier leading the second unit nodded and led his men down the dirt road. Kitt, meanwhile, set out along the footpath. The other two commandos followed, carbines at the ready, maintaining a ten-yard gap between them. To his right, Kitt could see what at first appeared to be a steep gorge, but as his eyes adjusted to the darkness he could make out a fence and was able to determine that they were walking alongside a quarry. When the cold breeze shifted, a foul stench wafted up from the pit, turning Kitt's stomach. He'd smelled a similar odor a few times before—it was unmistakable.

"Carrion," he whispered to himself. Rotting flesh.

When he came to a spot where the path veered closer to the lip of the chasm, Kitt detoured through a gap in the periphery fence and glanced downward. It was too dark for him to make out details, but he could see there was a small mound of some sort directly at the base of the drop-off. He was speculating as to what it might be when gunfire erupted downhill. As he turned in the direction of the sound, there was a follow-up crack of rifle fire from the rooftop of the nearby hut. Kitt groaned and nearly tumbled backward into the pit as a bullet plowed into his chest, just above the heart.

No, he thought to himself as he felt himself engulfed by a sudden, all-consuming darkness.

"WE'RE EN ROUTE as we speak," Bolan told Price over their secured long-distance connection. He was speaking from the cockpit of the Kiowa Warrior Grimaldi had just propelled back across the border into Afghanistan. Price was cloistered off to one side in the Computer Room back at Stony Man Farm, a delicate finger pressed to one ear to block out the sounds of the cyberteam laboring in the background.

"Be careful," Price replied. "Call me selfish, but I want you back in one piece."

"That makes two of us," Bolan replied. "Gotta go—we're closing in."

Price crossed the room and quickly updated the cybercrew on the rescue mission in Balqhat, concluding with news that the freed BBC filmmaker had taken footage of the captors, who'd included SVR agent Eshaq Faryad.

"Fantastic!" Kurtzman exclaimed once Price had finished her briefing. "Match that up with what they've got out of the interrogation room in Bagram, and we've got Moscow dead to rights on being in the thick of this."

"What'd they find out?" Price asked.

"Just came in," Kurtzman said. "That Afghan general who went stoolie has copped to Faryad being Russia's liaison between them and the Taliban."

"That's great news."

"Let's see the Kremlin try to wrangle off the hook now," Delahunt said.

"I'm sure they'll just issue another denial," Kurtzman predicted. "That or they'll say there's some other explanation. You know how it works."

"All too well," Delahunt said. "If Faryad had pulled off that massacre and put the footage out on Al Jazeera, we'd be the ones in the hot seat."

"And nobody'd believe us," Tokaido added.

"You're probably right," Price said. "We definitely dodged the bullet on that one."

"So now it's all down to Aden Saleh's safe house," Wethers said. Price nodded. "Striker should be there shortly."

"Bagram has gunships on the way," Kurtzman reported. "And there's already one chopper close by."

"I guess that leaves us on the sidelines," Delahunt said.

"We've done our part," Price replied, "but you're right. For now, it's out of our hands."

ROB KITT SLOWLY opened his eyes. He was confused and disoriented.

I'm still alive? he wondered.

The Special Ops captain could hear gunfire around him, and he was aware of the cold ground pressing against him and a sharp pain in his chest. He reached for his sternum, expecting to feel blood. Instead, his fingers brushed across a bullet hole in his shirt and then settled on the faint bulge of his cigarette case. He could feel an indentation in the case and realized his father's heirloom had just saved his life.

"Thanks, Dad," Kitt muttered faintly.

Once he'd regained his wits, Kitt shifted his position and glanced back toward the trail he'd strayed from before being shot. One of his men was lying facedown on the path, not moving. Nearby, the other member of his team crouched, M-16 planted against his shoulder as he traded shots with the enemy.

Kitt groped the ground beside him, trying to locate his carbine. It was nowhere in reach. Kitt realized it had to have dropped into the quarry when he was hit.

"Damn it!" he cursed.

Slowly he began to crawl away from the edge, hoping to get within reach of his fallen colleague's assault rifle. He hadn't gone far when the other soldier suddenly pitched to one side, taken out by a kill shot to the head. A barrage of follow-up rounds pounded the ground, inching toward Kitt. Still unarmed and with no other place to take cover, Kitt reflexively took the only option left to him. He crawled backward as fast as he could until he reached the drop-off. There, he turned slightly, dangling his feet down into the pit while pressing his upper torso against the edge. When the bullets raked closer, he eased back farther, lowering himself completely. He grabbed at the edge as he went down, but there was little to hold on to. After a few seconds he lost his grip and went into a free fall.

Landing at the base of the pit, Kitt's fall was partially broken by the mound he'd spotted earlier. He rolled on impact, clearing the heap. He was dazed and the stench of carrion nearly overcame him completely. He could see now that he'd landed on a pile of corpses. Some of them were human—none of them were intact.

Kitt slowly sat up, fighting off his nausea. He was trying to figure out his next move when he heard a noise in the darkness on the other side of the pit. It was a low, deep growl. He stared in the direction of the sound. Seconds later, a shadowy form padded out of the darkness on four legs. Soon there was a second growling, followed by the appearance of yet another creature. Snow leopards.

A cold fear seized Kitt. Now he understood what had caused the dismemberment of the bodies that lay around him. Fast on the heels of this grim epiphany came an even more troubling revelation.

I'm next, Kitt thought to himself.

23

Kitt stumbled backward, recoiling from the advancing creatures. His right hand brushed against something lying on the
ground next to him. It wasn't cold flesh or exposed bone. It
was metal.

His M-16.

One of the leopards snarled and was about to spring forward when Kitt swung his carbine into play. He fired high,
but the loud outburst echoing off the quarry walls sent the
big cats retreating back into the darkness.

Heart racing, Kitt rose to his feet and slowly backpedaled
until he brushed up against the sheer stone wall leading back
up to the ground. He kept his assault rifle trained on the shadows as he reached behind him, groping for possible handholds.
There were none.

Off in the darkness, above the distant reverberation of gun-
shots, Kitt heard the snarl of the cats. They were still out of
sight, but he could tell they were spreading out as if preparing
to come at him again from different directions.

"Smart move, kitties," he whispered, fighting back his
fear.

Kitt was weighing his chances against a follow-up attack
when the beam of a searchlight suddenly stabbed its way into
the quarry, illuminating the leopards. The cats froze, then
turned from the light, fleeing into the shelter of a cave on the
other side of the pit.

As the light beam swept across the quarry floor, exposing the half-eaten remains that had cushioned his fall, Kitt

glanced up and saw the outline of a helicopter drifting down toward him. Someone had climbed out onto the skid and was feeding out what looked to be a long rope. Moments later, Bolan leaped clear of the chopper, dropping a few yards, then began to lower himself, hand over hand, down a length of the same rappelling line he'd used during the rescue mission in Balqhat.

"How about we take you off the menu here," the Executioner called out once he'd brought himself down to within ten feet of Kitt.

"No argument here," Kitt shouted back.

The Special Ops commando ventured from the quarry wall, extending one hand upward while still keeping his carbine aimed toward the snow leopards. The big cats were poised at the mouth of the cave, and only seconds after Bolan had clasped his fingers around Kitt's wrist, they ventured forth, ready to make another move toward their prey. Kitt gave them pause with another warning blast, then quickly slung the carbine over his shoulder, freeing his other hand to grab hold of the rappel line.

"Okay, we're out of here!" Bolan said, giving the line a tug. Up in the cockpit, Grimaldi responded, guiding the Kiowa back up into the night. Kitt exhaled with relief as his feet left the quarry floor and he could feel himself being lifted up.

As they rose from the pit, Bolan and Kitt glanced down at the cats and the corpses that had been cast down for them to feast on.

"I'm not positive, but I think one of those bodies is O'Brien's," Kitt called out to Bolan.

"We'll have to come back for him," Bolan said. "We're not out of this yet."

24

Saleh had already decided it wasn't safe to remain in the hut when he heard a thump overhead. The guard who'd climbed up to use the roof as a sniper post had just been struck down. As the body rolled down the incline and tumbled to the ground outside the hut, the Taliban leader rushed across the room and swept his arm across the low table, toppling both Yung's notebook computer and O'Brien's microcomputer to the floor.

"What good did that do?" Yung shouted at Saleh.

"We need to get out of here!" he snapped. Saleh grabbed the edge of the table and overturned it, revealing a trapdoor lying flush with the dirt floor. He yanked the door open and began to lower himself down a ladder built into the vertical shaft.

"What about him?" Yung asked, pointing at Pradhan.

"Get rid of him!" Saleh said before disappearing down the shaft.

"Gladly." Yung turned on the Afghan, reaching for his pistol. "I've been waiting for this."

Pradhan stared silently at Yung, any hope of seeing his wife again fading before his eyes. Why had it come to this? he wondered.

Yung raised his pistol and was about to fire when the front door burst inward. It was Kitt, M-16 in hand. Yung whirled and shifted aim. Kitt beat him to the draw, obliterating the Uzbekistan's midsection with 5.56 mm NATO rounds. Yung plunged forward, landing facedown at Pradhan's feet.

Kitt charged forward and pressed a thumb to Yung's neck, checking for a pulse he knew he wouldn't find. As he did so, he glanced up at Pradhan.

"You're the one who sent out that video."

He just nodded.

"Good work," Kitt told him.

Pradhan wasn't interested in compliments. "My wife," he said. "She was taken to Balqhat with some others from—"

"She's fine. So are the others," Kitt said. His gaze drifted to the trapdoor, which had dropped back into place. "Did someone just use that?"

Pradhan nodded. "Their leader."

Kitt bolted past the overturned table and grabbed the trapdoor's handle. When he tried to pull it open, the door wouldn't budge.

"Must've locked it from the other side," Kitt said. He stood back and took aim with his M-16, rattling off enough rounds to chew apart the thick wood. As he pried at the loose pieces, creating an opening large enough to squeeze through, he assured Pradhan, "I'll be back. He can't have gotten too far."

As HE NEARED the first bend in the tunnel, Saleh paused and glanced back. Someone had just cleared the vertical shaft he'd taken moments before to escape from the hut. He assumed it was Yung.

"Hurry!" he shouted.

Saleh was answered by the staccato barkings of an assault rifle. One of the rounds burrowed into his shoulder while the others skimmed off the rock walls of the tunnel. The Taliban leader roared in pain as he stumbled around the corner, clutching the wound. Livid, he reached out with his good arm and pulled hard on a lever jutting from the wall. With a loud screech, a thick metal plate dropped from an overhead cavity. The ground beneath Saleh's feet quaked slightly as the plate slammed into place, creating a barrier between him and his assailant. Saleh remembered his men scoffing at his desire to create extra safeguards within the tunnels around the safe house after they'd been chiseled out. He knew at the time that it was wise to take such precautions, and now his foresight had paid off. He still had a chance to get away.

WHILE KITT HAD ELECTED to fight on the ground as soon as he'd been pulled from the quarry, Bolan had returned to the chopper's cockpit. It had been a round from his M-16 that had taken out the sniper atop the roof of Saleh's hut. As Grimaldi guided the Kiowa out over the opium field, the Executioner was directing his fire at Taliban fighters trading shots with the surviving members of Kitt's Special Ops team. The aerial assault had been joined by Kitt's chopper and, less than a mile away, Bolan could see a pair of Apache gunships swooping down toward the battlefield.

"Take out the sod house!" Bolan told Grimaldi, pointing out the low building at the edge of the planting field. Two more gunners had just charged out of the structure.

"On it."

Grimaldi lined up the chopper and moments later a Hellfire missile surged from the Kiowa's exterior weapons pylon. The warhead detonated once it crashed through the front doorway of the outbuilding, laying waste to several enemy soldiers as well as a cache of explosives that amplified the blast enough to bring down the sod roof. Grimaldi surveyed his handiwork as he passed over the collapsed structure, then banked to his left and followed the dirt road leading back up to the helipad. Beside him, Bolan scanned the grounds for more targets and spotted two of Kitt's men sprawled dead where they'd been hit during the onset of the firefight. Aside from Kitt, that left only one commando of the original six still in the fight, but with the Apaches now on the scene, it seemed clear that the Taliban had met their match.

"Set me down on the helipad, then go ahead and make another pass," Bolan told Grimaldi.

"Will do," Grimaldi said.

Bolan's intention was to inspect the truck standing idle at the top of the road, but as they cleared the rise, his plans changed when he spotted someone moving through the shadows in the back of the large cave concealing the helipad. Saleh had just emerged from his underground escape route and was making his way toward an untended ATV.

"I see him," Grimaldi said, transferring one hand to the controls for the Kiowa's fixed forward machine gun. A stream of .50-caliber rounds thundered into the cave, but not before Saleh had a chance to dive for cover behind the ATV. The slugs tore apart the balloon tires and hammered the vehicle's chassis, but Saleh had made it safely out of the line of fire.

"My turn," Bolan said.

The Kiowa was close enough that the Executioner was able to leap clear and land on his feet at the outer edge of the helipad. Blood trailing down his wounded shoulder, Saleh leaned out from behind the ATV and fired his Ruger. Bolan had dropped to a crouch and the rounds streaked past him, glancing off the helicopter behind him. Bolan fought off an urge to dive for cover and instead charged forward, M-16 blazing.

The shots missed Saleh, who had again ducked back behind the ATV, then bolted clear, racing toward the tunnel through which Kitt had reached the cave. If he could make it that far, the Taliban leader felt he'd be able to lose his pursuer in the labyrinth of subterranean passageways. It was a risky move, however, as he was forced to place himself back in the line of fire. The gambit failed, and he'd only made it a few yards into the opening before Bolan brought him down with another autoburst.

When he reached the ATV, Bolan hunched over, bracing for return fire—but it didn't come. The Executioner cautiously peered over the top of the vehicle, then moved clear of it and warily approached the Taliban leader. Saleh writhed on the ground, more blood seeping through fresh wounds in his upper back. He was still clutching his pistol, but when he stared over his shoulder and spotted Bolan he cast the gun aside.

"I surrender," the Taliban leader groaned as he struggled to his knees, trembling.

Bolan kept his assault rifle trained on Saleh and told him, "Hands on your head."

Saleh nodded and slowly raised his arms, grimacing at the pain in his shoulder. Once his hands were clasped atop his head, he began to stand up.

"Stay where you are," Bolan commanded.

Saleh partially obliged, stopping only to raise his right knee so that he had one foot on the ground. He wavered, struggling for balance, then pitched to one side reaching out as if to grab the tunnel wall for support. Bolan saw through the ruse and fired his last rounds, striking Saleh in the chest as his fingers were closing around a lever identical to the one he'd pulled back in the tunnel beneath his headquarters. Death claimed the Taliban leader, but as he fell, he tripped the lever. A thick metal plate, much like the other one, dropped down through an overhead slot in the tunnel ceiling. This time, however, the ploy failed its objective. Saleh had fallen into the plate's path, and it crashed down on his neck with enough brute force to decapitate him. The ground shuddered a moment, and when it stopped Bolan found himself staring at the severed head, which lay faceup at the base of the plate, three inches of metal separating it from the rest of Saleh's body.

Out on the helipad, Grimaldi set down the Kiowa and scrambled out. When he caught up with Bolan and spotted the severed head, he glanced away.

"Ouch," he said. "That's one hell of a way to go."

Bolan said nothing. He continued to stare at Saleh's grisly visage, unsettled by more than its eerie, lifeless countenance. He suspected that with the man's death, the Taliban had been dealt a major blow in their effort to wreak mayhem not only in Afghanistan but across the globe. The sight of the severed head also stirred up a distant memory that took him back to a high-school mythology class in his native Pittsfield, when he'd been morbidly enthralled by the tale of Hydra, a beast with regenerative powers so great that if its head were to be chopped off, two more would grow in its place. So it was with the Taliban, Bolan knew.

"Okay, sideshow's over," Grimaldi said, noting the dark, brooding look in Bolan's eyes. "We might be able to get in a few more licks out there, but I think we've got 'em beat."

Bolan turned to his colleague and spoke in a voice weary from a lifetime of battling the Hydras of the modern world.

"I'm not so sure about that...."

TAKE 'EM FREE
2 action-packed novels plus a mystery bonus

NO RISK
NO OBLIGATION TO BUY

JAMES AXLER

DEATH LANDS®

Doom Helix

A new battle for Deathlands has begun...

The Deathlands feudal system may be hell on earth but it must be protected from invaders from Shadow Earth, a parallel world stripped clean of its resources by the ruling conglomerate and its white coats. Ryan and his band had a near-fatal encounter with them once before and now these superhuman predators are back, ready to topple the hellscape's baronies one by one.

Available September wherever books are sold.